"I'm finding this platonic proximity a bit of a strain."

Reed looked around pointedly at the bedroom they shared. "Are you going to be able to go back to working for me after this?"

It would be difficult going back to just being employer and secretary, their relationship possessing an air of intimacy now that wasn't all pretense. But Darcy couldn't imagine *not* working for him, seeing him every day.

"I'm sure I can," she replied awkwardly. "After all, we're only sharing a room."

"Bringing you here was a mistake. If only I'd realized my family would expect us to sleep together! But I need you here, Darcy." This last seemed to be added almost to himself.

She would walk barefoot through a pit of snakes if he asked her to. But she wasn't sure staying on here wasn't going to be even more lethal.

CAROLE MORTIMER, one of our most popular—and prolific—English authors, began writing for the Harlequin Presents series in 1979. She now has more than forty top-selling romances to her credit and shows no signs whatsoever of running out of plot ideas. She writes strong traditional romances with a distinctly modern appeal, and her winning way with characters and romantic plot twists has earned her an enthusiastic audience worldwide.

Books by Carole Mortimer

HARLEQUIN PRESENTS

HARLEQUIN SIGNATURE EDITION

These books may be available at your local bookseller.

Don't miss any of our special offers. Write to us at the following address for information on our newest releases.

Harlequin Reader Service
901 Fuhrmann Blvd., P.O. Box 1397, Buffalo, NY 14240
Canadian address: P.O. Box 603,
Fort Erie, Ont. L2A 9Z9

CAROLE MORTIMER

glass slippers and unicorns

Harlequin Books

TORONTO • NEW YORK • LONDON
AMSTERDAM • PARIS • SYDNEY • HAMBURG
STOCKHOLM • ATHENS • TOKYO • MILAN

For John,
Matthew and Joshua

Harlequin Presents first edition December 1986
ISBN 0-373-10939-3

Original hardcover edition published in 1986
by Mills & Boon Limited

CHAPTER ONE

'For God's sake, Darcy, I know you're always losing things; but my mother!'

Put like that it did sound a little careless. But it wasn't completely accurate. She hadn't exactly lost Maud Hunter; misplaced her was a better way of describing what had happened, she thought.

But Reed didn't look as if he wanted to hear that right now, and Darcy doubted he would find the distinction at all reassuring. After all, she *had* gone to the airport to meet Maud Hunter, and she *had* returned without her and now had no idea where she could be!

Reed stood up in a forceful movement. 'My God, Darcy, you lost my *mother!*'

She sighed, pulling a face at his incredulity. 'You already said that.'

Sparks flew in accusing green eyes, his mouth tight. 'And I'll say it again, too, as many damned times as I have to to be able to take it in!' He paced the room with long legs, his movements not made with their usual fluidity but with spasmodic energy. 'You lost a sixty-year-old woman who's just endured a long flight and is on her first trip to England in ten years!' It wasn't a question but a statement of fact. 'This is a human being I'm talking about here, Darcy,' he growled.

'Not one of those dozen left shoes sitting in the bottom of your closet—and this is not the time for you to point out that closet means something else over here,' he snarled as she opened her mouth to speak, satisfaction gleaming in his eyes as she quickly closed it again. '... Dozen left shoes sitting in the bottom of your closet,' he repeated hardly, 'because you have somehow lost the right ones!'

'It's the right shoes in the wardrobe and the left ones lost,' she nervously corrected; Reed hardly ever lost his temper, but she knew that right now he had, his whole body tensed with it. Well she *had* misplaced his mother between here and Heathrow. Or did she mean Heathrow and here——

'Darcy!' he grated between clenched teeth. 'I don't give a damn if it's half a dozen of each——'

'I thought you were trying to stop swearing?' She frowned as he used the word twice in as many minutes after days of holding back his usual habit of cursing whenever something didn't go exactly as he planned it should.

'Darcy!' Her name came out as a fierce guttural growl this time. 'A saint would swear at a time like this,' he added in exasperation as she looked at him with bewildered confusion.

A saint was something they both knew he wasn't. As a professional speculator—in just about anything!—he often didn't have the time to wait around and be pleasant. Admittedly he was dealing mainly in shares at the moment, but even so he was ruthless, was first and foremost a businessman. He was also very successful at what he did. The only way that Darcy could see he might possibly have fallen down on that success was hiring her as his secretary! And she had a feeling he felt the same way at the moment.

He looked at her with sharp green eyes, stopping his pacing. 'I suppose you did actually meet her at the airport?' he asked hopefully.

'Of course I did,' she protested indignantly.

Reed eyed her suspiciously. 'Are you sure?'

Her mouth compressed. 'She's a short lady, about my height, I suppose,' she frowned thoughtfully, 'with curly white hair, and green eyes like yours.'

'I told you all that before you left for the airport,' he snapped impatiently.

'I have her luggage downstairs in the boot of the car!' Darcy told him exasperatedly. She might have a habit of losing things, but she certainly didn't invent meeting people. 'She told me all about how naughty you were as a little boy,' she remembered, her eyes dancing merrily. 'How you turned the hose on the——'

'All right,' Reed barked irritably, obviously not in the mood to reminisce about his mischievous childhood. 'I'll accept that you did meet my mother——'

'Well thanks!' she bit out caustically, glaring at him.

'But what the hell have you done with her now?'

Reed had such a deep timbre of voice that when he raised it you felt like putting a hand on all the breakable objects in the room in case they clattered from their resting place and shattered on the ground. She saw his eyes narrow as she winced, clasping her hands together in front of her to resist the urge.

'I haven't done anything with her, Reed,' she denied wearily. 'On the drive back she mentioned it was years since she had read an English newspaper, and when she fell asleep——'

'You calmly parked the car and went off to buy her one,' he finished disgustedly.

Her eyes blazed deeply blue. 'I was only gone a couple of minutes!'

'Long enough for my mother to disappear!'

'Will you stop saying that as if you think I had something to do with it!' she protested, frowning heavily as his raised eyebrows seemed to say, 'Well, didn't you?' 'When I came back out of the shop with the newspaper, she had gone,' Darcy defended.

'That was over an hour ago.' He glared at her. 'And you had no right going off and leaving her like that.'

'I didn't think she could come to any harm just sitting in the car.' Darcy glared right back.

At least, she tried to glare. She was sure it didn't come out quite as fierce as it was meant to do, though, as she squinted slightly to bring her myopic vision into focus enough to read Reed's expression.

Reed seemed to stiffen even more as he saw that squint. 'Did you forget to put your contacts in again?' he asked suspiciously.

'No, I didn't forget!' she snapped, the guilty flush that coloured her cheeks giving the instant lie to that statement. 'I just haven't had time to put them in yet! I was late getting up, and then as soon as I arrived you told me I had to go and meet your mother, and——'

'Great,' he ground out fiercely. 'This is just *great*! I can see it all now.' He raised his head to look at the ceiling, taking deep controlling breaths. 'It probably wasn't even *my* mother you met. The poor woman probably realised that after a while and made her escape at the first opportunity.'

Darcy stood up indignantly, too angered by his scornful tone to want to admit to the vanity of wearing her rarely used glasses to go to the airport to meet his mother, but of having taken them off only seconds ago before she entered the office, not wanting Reed to see her wearing the heavy dark frames. 'You're being very unfair, Reed.'

'Am I?' he scorned, shaking his head. 'I don't think so.'

'As it's obvious you have so little confidence in my ability to do anything right, I don't know why you ever sent me to meet your mother,' she accused emotionally.

'I was unavoidably tied up here; there was no one else *but* you to send!'

She gave a shaky gasp. 'Then maybe you should never have employed me!'

'I wouldn't have done, but I thought the rest of the business world needed saving from itself!' he rasped disgustedly.

Tears instantly made her vision more blurred. 'My qualifications are good——'

'But anyone who turns up for an interview as a secretary at nine o'clock at night——'

'That was the time your letter said!' she protested agitatedly.

Reed gave a disgusted snort. 'It was because my temporary secretary was so incompetent that I needed another permanent secretary! No woman turns up for an interview for a secretary's position at nine o'clock at night unless the prospective employer has more than just secretarial duties in mind and she's decided she's agreeable to that—or she's just plain stupid!' he finished contemptuously.

It was so obvious which one he thought she was! 'I'd only been in London a couple of months; this was only my fourth interview!'

'No woman in her right mind turns up for an interview in a deserted office building at nine o'clock at night!' Reed maintained forcefully. 'Not even a woman from the provinces! I can still remember the look on the night security man's face when I came in answer to his call that you were here demanding to see me, saying that you had an appointment!'

Darcy was sure the colour in her cheeks was going to remain a permanent fixture as Reed seemed intent on recalling all the stupid things she had done since the moment they had met so awkwardly. Of course she had thought it strange that Reed Hunter wanted to interview her at nine o'clock at night, but it had been her first time in

London after living the last twenty-two and a half years with her parents in a village that was so small even the locals said it could be missed if you blinked as you were approaching it! The only two jobs she had had since leaving school six years earlier had been in the small town three miles away; she had just assumed things were done differently in the capital. How was she supposed to know Reed's temporary secretary had made a typing error and it should have read a.m. in the letter and not p.m.? Reed must have read the letter through before signing it; he should have spotted the mistake, too. Although once again she didn't think he would appreciate her pointing that out to him just now!

'I still got the job, didn't I?' she reminded him resentfully.

'As I said——'

'You thought the business world needed saving from itself,' she finished emotionally.

He nodded. 'And I was intrigued by your name,' he admitted reluctantly.

Bewildered eyes the colour of cornflowers opened wider than ever. 'My name?' she repeated incredulously.

Reed nodded again, impatiently this time. 'That was why you were the first person scheduled for interview that morning.' He gave a pointed sigh at his mention of the time of day she should have been here. 'Your qualifications were also a little better than the other applicants', but it was your name that intrigued me. Hell, I wasn't even sure if Darcy Faversham was a man or a woman!'

'You employed me because of my *name*?' Darcy said again, incredulously.

'It gave you the edge,' he confirmed irritably. 'As I said, the other three applicants were almost as well qualified.'

'I can't believe this,' she said dazedly.

'Oh, believe it,' he rasped. 'Once I'd met you I should have known better!'

'You make a living by gambling on hunches,' she reminded him dully, stunned by what he had just told her. To think that if her name had been plain Susan Smith she wouldn't have got the job! 'And this time it let you down.' She straightened her shoulders defensively. 'I'll leave——'

'Not until we've found my mother you won't,' he cut in fiercely. 'Forget about your damned pride for a moment and try and help me think where she could be!'

Pride. Yes, her pride was hurt. But so was she. She knew she had a habit of losing things, but she only lost them because she forgot what she had done with them. But her work had always been unquestionably competent, and Reed could never accuse her of ever losing anything of his.

Except his mother, she realised with a wince.

But you couldn't lose people, not really; they had a habit, adults at least, of always turning up again. She felt sure Maud Hunter would be no exception.

She chewed thoughtfully on her bottom lip. 'She took her handbag with her——'

'She did?' Reed pounced, narrow-eyed.

Darcy nodded. 'Yes——'

'Then at least she isn't wandering about London completely penniless too!'

She wasn't a violent woman, believing that passivity often achieved the same results, but if Reed continued to act as if she had thrust the equivalent of a new-born chick into a pack of wolves she knew she wasn't going to be able to stop the urge her hand had to slap him across one lean cheek.

He wasn't a handsome man by any standards, but that he was attractive couldn't be doubted, with his hair thick and dark, almost black in some lights, brows the same colour jutting out over eyes of luminous green, a slight bump to the straightness of his nose where it had been broken playing American football during his teens, his mouth often snapping words too cutting for the sensuousness of his bottom lip to be noticed. Although, from the amount of women who telephoned him at the office, it was noticeable enough! He was well over six feet tall, and still had the physique that could have taken him into pro-football if the challenge of speculation hadn't been the stronger of the two.

He towered at least a foot over Darcy as she faced him, his stance threatening even if she knew he would never physically hurt her. He was a hawk, why should he bother himself with the little mouse? Even if the mouse did occasionally, very occasionally, roar!

'Reed, she'll turn up——'

'Will she?' he scorned. 'It's been almost two hours, and she hasn't "turned up" yet!'

That guilty blush returned to her cheeks. 'The police——'

'Will not look for a woman who's only been missing two hours!' he snapped disgustedly.

She chewed on her inner lip, oblivious to the soreness she was inflicting, not knowing what else to say. Because she didn't think Maud Hunter *was* missing, was sure the other woman would make her way here or to Reed's apartment when she was good and ready. But until she did, Reed wasn't going to calm down.

And in the meantime she had given him her notice. She was regretting that pride-saving impulse already. He was an interesting man to work for, no two days the same, the heavy workload keeping her occupied long outside the nine until five she was supposed to work. And that suited her. But she knew Reed would never forgive her for this, that he obviously adored his mother.

The day had begun so nicely, too; birthday cards from her family and friends pushed through her letter box by the postman, a couple of parcels left on her doorstep. She was twenty-three today, felt as if she were finally putting the past behind her. And now this. It wouldn't just be the work she would miss.

'Darcy, are you listening to me!'

She gave a surprised start as Reed shouted at her. Concentrate on one thing at a time, they had told her. And she had. And it had worked. But now, more than two years later, she still had difficulty giving her attention to more than one thing at any given moment. Whatever Reed had been saying to her, she hadn't heard him. And she could see by the angry glitter in his fierce eyes that he knew that.

'I said,' he ground out between clenched teeth, 'I think the best thing to do is drive back to where you parked your car and look around there for her. Can you remember where that was?'

Her mouth tightened at his obvious scorn. 'Of course I can. There's nothing wrong with my memory——'

'Because you don't have one!'

'Reed!' she gasped her hurt surprise; he had never been deliberately cruel to her before.

He put his hands up in apology. 'OK, that was uncalled for,' he acknowledged grimly. 'I'm upset, and I'm taking it out on you. But I'm damned worried.' He frowned.

She could see that, had never seen him this agitated before. But she also knew that if she mentioned it he would point out that he had never lost his mother before!

'Don't you think one of us should remain here?' she suggested practically. 'Just in case she should come here.'

He thought for a moment before nodding. 'You stay,' he bit out. 'I couldn't stand the inactivity right now.' He took his jacket off the back of his chair, shrugging in to it. 'And for goodness' sake go and put your contacts in so that you'll at least recognise it is her if she arrives!'

She hurried into the adjoining office, leaving the door open for him to follow, groaning her dismay as the outer door opened and a grinning Marc Kincaid came in. 'Not now, Marc,' she said, trying to push him back outside the door before Reed saw him. 'Reed isn't in the mood to see you right now,' she explained frantically as Marc looked down at her in surprise, her efforts to evict him proving ineffectual, Marc being almost as big as Reed.

'He's never in the mood to see me,' Marc dismissed, easily standing his ground. 'But——'

'He wants to see you even less than usual today.' Darcy threw a hunted look over her shoulder; Reed was, thankfully, still in his office. Although her luck couldn't hold. It hadn't so far today! 'Please leave, Marc,' she begged him desperately.

'He *will* want to see me, Darcy,' he assured her. 'But how about a kiss first?' he encouraged huskily, bending his head to claim her mouth with his.

It was far from the first kiss she had shared with this wickedly handsome man; she was still slightly amazed that someone as attractive and popular as he was wanted to date her. He was handsome enough to have any woman he wanted, with his thick blond hair, dancing blue eyes, a seductively smiling mouth, the masculinity of his body undoubted in his tight denims and fitted blue shirt. But for the last six weeks he had asked to see her every night. Not that she had accepted every night, but four out of seven still amounted to a lot of nights.

And Reed was going to be even more furious

than he already was if he found him here. She
had met Marc because Reed had become his
financial partner in the photographic studio he
ran on a lower floor of the building, but Reed
didn't approve of *their* personal relationship
spilling over into his office.

'And just what happens if someone wants to
come in the door?' grated an icy voice.

Marc lifted his head slowly, in no hurry to
release Darcy as he looked up to grin at the other
man. 'They either ask us to move or wait until
we're finished,' he drawled unconcernedly.

'Marc——'

'Darcy tells me you're in a bad mood,' he
continued as if she hadn't tried to cut in.
'Something wrong, Reed?' he held Darcy snugly
against his side, his arm about her shoulders.

'Yes, something is wrong,' the other man
hissed. 'I'll leave Darcy to tell you all about it!'

Marc still blocked the doorway. 'Maybe I can
help?' His eyes gleamed with amusement.

'I doubt it,' Reed snapped, shooting Darcy a
disparaging look.

'Sure?' Marc taunted.

'Marc, please,' she groaned, as Reed looked
ready to explode if the other man didn't get out
of his way. 'Reed is in a hurry.'

'Too much of one for his visitor?' Marc
challenged.

'Is this important?' Reed snapped tersely.

Marc grinned. 'I think so. I think you will, too,
if you stop long enough to listen to me.'

'Can't it wait?' Reed sighed impatiently.

'I doubt it.' The other man shook his head mysteriously.

'Marc, unless it's really important please leave it until later.' She looked up at him pleadingly. 'You see, Reed's mother arrived in London this morning, and I——'

'I know,' he nodded.

'. . . lost her between here and Heathrow, and— What do you mean, you know?' Darcy frowned up at him as she realised what he had said; Reed went rigid with tension as he looked at the other man with narrowed eyes.

'I mean, I know that Maud arrived from America this morning.' Marc at last released her. 'You see, I was just on my way out to lunch when I noticed the lady peering up at the notice-board downstairs —and she had a long way to peer, believe me,' he teased. 'Anyway, being the helpful soul that I am, I asked her if I could be of any help.' He raised mocking brows at Reed. 'She looked too young and beautiful to be your mother, old chap,' he mocked. 'But she assures me that's who she is.'

'What have you done with her?' Reed demanded harshly.

'Nothing, she's right outside.' Marc shrugged, as if he couldn't understand what all the fuss was about.

Reed pushed him aside none too gently, coming to an abrupt halt as the tiny lady causing all the uproar appeared in the doorway.

'Hello, darling.' She reached up to kiss her eldest son on the cheek. 'I was just admiring your lovely nameplate on the wall outside. You——'

'Mother!'

'Mrs Hunter!'

She blinked lids over surprised green eyes as Reed and Darcy spoke at the same time. 'Yes, dears?' she prompted interestedly, giving Darcy a chiding look as she did so. 'I'm sure I asked you to call me Maud,' she scolded, coming further into the room. 'My, this is a nice office, Reed,' she said admiringly as she looked around. 'Do you——'

'Mother, where the hell have you been?' he bit out with controlled violence, his hands clenched at his sides.

She blinked again, obviously surprised by his vehemence. 'Darling, you know I don't like it when you swear——'

'Not another one!' he ground out exasperatedly, momentarily closing his eyes, the glitter even more intense when he raised his lids. 'Mother, you disappeared from Darcy's car two hours ago, where have you been?' he demanded, the flame in his eyes positively primitive as Marc gave a chuckle at his omission of 'the hell' the second time around. Marc's expression instantly became bland.

Darcy gave him a warning look. Ordinarily the two men were quite good friends, although on the surface they had little in common but their intense professionalism and an eye for beautiful women. Marc was completely dedicated to his work, was a perfectionist, and in a different way Reed was the same about his investments. Their approach to women was different, however, Marc being a different man then, light and frivolous, whereas Reed never let anyone too close to him, not even the women he took as his lovers. Maybe they weren't so different in that respect after all: being light and frivolous didn't allow for deeper relationships either! But it was obvious Reed didn't appreciate Marc's levity now, although from Marc's wink in her direction he wasn't too worried about it.

Maud's expression seemed to say she didn't know what all the fuss was about either. 'I had a nice rest in Darcy's car after the flight; I had the misfortune to be seated next to a man on the plane who just would not stop talking,' she said disgustedly. 'He talked all the way over here— when he wasn't drinking,' she added with a frown. 'Do you know that he——'

'*Mother!*'

'I wish you would let me tell this in my own way, Reed,' his mother admonished sternly. 'You know how I forget things when I'm constantly interrupted— Did you say something, dear?' She looked concernedly at Darcy as she made a choking sound.

'No! Er—no,' she repeated lamely.

Green eyes twinkled at her from a face still beautiful, not marred by the usual worry lines of a woman her age. And Darcy was beginning to realise why! Why hadn't she noticed at the airport? Probably because she had been too busy trying to see where she was going to notice just how vague Maud Hunter was!

Maud turned back to her son. 'As I was

saying,' she said pointedly. 'I was very tired after the flight. And then this nice young lady met me at the airport.' She beamed at Darcy. 'She's such a nice girl, Reed. I hope you're good to her.' She frowned. 'Anyway,' she hastily continued as her son looked as if he might explode again, 'when I woke up I realised Darcy must have been kind enough to let me continue sleeping, and then when I got out of the car to look for her I couldn't find her. It's strange the things that come back to you, you know,' she told them all, 'because I suddenly realised I was very close to where my old friend Joyce Bennett use to live. After ten years I still remembered——'

'Mother,' Reed cut in on her ramblings in a strained voice. 'You aren't going to tell us that you calmly went off to visit a friend while Darcy was frantically trying to find you?'

'Were you, dear?' Maud looked at her concernedly. 'I am sorry. You see, I——'

'Mother, *please!*'

Darcy completely sympathised with Reed's impatience this time; she felt like shaking the muddle-headed woman herself!

Maud sighed. 'I went back to the car when I couldn't find Darcy, but that had disappeared as well, and that was when I——'

'Went off to visit your old friend Joyce Bennett,' Reed finished icily.

Maud looked bewildered by his anger. 'Well— yes. But——'

'Didn't you realise that Darcy would be worried about you? That *I* would be worried about you when she arrived back here without you?'

'I didn't mean to be gone quite as long as I was,' she grimaced. 'Once Joyce and I started talking——'

'I'm sure,' Reed grated. 'I think you owe Darcy an apology—I think we *both* do!'

'You do?' His mother frowned. 'I hope you haven't been shouting at her, Reed,' she rebuked. 'It wasn't Darcy's fault that I was late getting here.'

'I'm beginning to see that,' he sighed heavily. 'Let's go through to my office, Mother. I'll talk to you later, Darcy.' It was an order, not a request.

'Can you believe that?' Marc chuckled as he sat on the edge of Darcy's desk once they were alone. 'That sweet little old lady, Reed the Rake's mother!'

'He isn't a rake.' Darcy automatically corrected Marc's nickname for her employer, while busily tidying the papers on her desk-top that had no need of it; her desk was always completely organised. 'And yes, I can believe she's his mother.' No two people who weren't related could have eyes of such a deep green. But other than those eyes the two had no similarities whatsoever!

'Sounds like he's going to have his hands full.' Marc still grinned.

'She's only here until tomorrow,' Darcy supplied absently. 'Reed is driving her down to Southampton then to get on her cruise-ship.' He had told her that much before she left for the airport this morning, although he had told her little else about his charming but vague mother.

'That's what I could do with, a nice long cruise.' Marc stretched lazily. 'I don't suppose you would care to come away with me this weekend?'

Her brows rose mockingly at his teasing expression. 'I don't suppose I would,' she drawled.

He grimaced his disappointment. 'I thought not. So, how is my birthday girl?'

Birthday girl; this was the worst day she had known in a long time! 'She's fine,' she lied, having forgotten that it *was* her birthday. 'She is also busy,' she added pointedly.

He stood up, holding up his hands defensively. 'I was only doing my good deed for the day——'

'I know.' She sighed at her lack of gratitude for the fact that he had safely delivered Maud to Reed. 'I'm sorry.' She gave him a tight smile. 'It's been chaotic here the last few hours, and——'

'Reed been throwing his weight around, has he?' Marc sympathised.

'Only a little.' She grimaced at the understatement. 'And he had the right.'

'Want to talk about it?' he encouraged softly.

Darcy shook her head, feeling too shaken to go into the details of her argument with Reed. 'Maybe tonight.' She shrugged.

'Ah yes, tonight.' Marc's eyes lit up excitedly. 'Put your glad rags on because tonight I have a surprise for you!'

She warily searched the glow of his eyes. 'What sort of surprise?'

He tapped the end of her nose playfully. 'If I tell you it won't be a surprise any more. Just do what little there is to improve on that beautiful face and wear your sexiest dress.'

'Beautiful face', Darcy thought despondently a short time later as she looked in the mirror she had used to finally put her contact lenses in. Marc photographed beautiful women all day long, and no one in their right mind could compare her to the multitude of beauties that went into his studio each day. But then, when had Marc ever claimed to be in his right mind?

She looked critically at her reflection, at the bubbly red-gold curls that refused to be tamed, deep blue eyes that seemed to have taken on a permanently vague look, a short nose liberally sprinkled with freckles even during the winter months, a pretty smiling mouth, with a dimple in her elfin chin. No make-up in the world could make her appear sophisticated and worldly; in fact it had the opposite effect, making her look garishly childish. She had been told once that her long dark lashes framing deep blue eyes were her best feature, and so the only affectation she did have was the use of contact lenses rather than glasses, although even that effect was ruined when she forgot to put them in, looking owlishly bewildered then. No wonder Reed lost all patience with her!

'Marc gone?' he suddenly rasped behind her.

Darcy jumped guiltily at being caught staring

at her reflection, hastily putting the mirror away in her bag, embarrassed by the apparent vanity. She nodded, not quite able to meet Reed's gaze. 'He was going to lunch, remember?' she dismissed lightly.

His mouth twisted. 'I'm surprised you didn't go with him!'

'I thought I had better wait around and see if you wanted me to clear out my desk and leave now or if you want me to stay on until you have my replacement.' She moistened her lips nervously, finally looking up at him, able to see him clearly for the first time today. He looked as forbidding as she had imagined he would! 'Maybe an incompetent secretary who doesn't possess a memory is better than none at all; I don't know.' She shrugged.

The hard lines of his face tightened even more. 'I was angry when I said that, Darcy,' he grated. 'I didn't mean it.'

'Didn't you?' she said dully, knowing that at the time he had said it he had meant every word.

'No.' He grimaced, moving to stand next to her desk. 'You're a damned good secretary, better than I——' He broke off, sighing impatiently.

'Better than you ever thought I would be,' Darcy finished for him ruefully. 'I manage, as long as I only concentrate on one thing at a time,' she added bitterly.

'Darcy——'

'At least, I thought I was quite competent.' She frowned uncertainly.

'You are,' Reed acknowledged forcefully. 'Hell,

I'm not making a very good job of this apology.'
He ran a hand through his already tousled black
hair. 'My only defence for my behaviour towards
you earlier is that I was worried out of my mind.'
He gave a weary sigh. 'You've seen my mother at
her worst; you can guess why!'

Yes, she could guess why, quite easily. Reed
was a man who made important decisions in a
matter of seconds, who gambled on the Stock
Exchange in millions rather than hundreds, and
his mother's vagueness must be quite an irritation
to such a man. But how could she explain to him
that her own forgetfulness had been acquired and
wasn't part of her fundamental character? She
couldn't do it without going into the past, and so
she knew she would never tell him.

'Does this mean you don't want me to leave?'
She frowned.

'Of course I don't want you to leave,' he
dismissed impatiently. 'Do you accept my
apology?'

Now wasn't the time to point out that he
hadn't actually got around to making one, not if
she wanted to continue working for him. And she
did want to continue doing that, very much.

'Of course.' She smiled her forgiveness. 'Would
you like me to take your mother to your
apartment now? I'm sure she would like to rest.'

'She would.' He nodded tersely. 'But I'll take
her.' His expression darkened as her eyes
shadowed over with pain. 'It has nothing to do
with the fact that between the two of you you
would probably forget where you're going,' he

refuted impatiently. 'As she only has today in England this end of her trip, I think I should spend a little time with her.'

'Of course,' Darcy acknowledged non-committally.

'Darcy——'

'Reed, could we go to Harrods on the way to your apartment?' His mother came out of his office. 'I want to buy some tea to take back with me.'

'Wouldn't it be better if you waited until you get back from the cruise before doing that?' he suggested after shooting a resigned look in Darcy's direction. 'You won't need it until then.'

'I suppose not.' She nodded thoughtfully, going to the door he held open for her. 'Maybe we can look at the coffee instead?' she suggested hopefully.

'Doesn't the same thing apply?' he pointed out drily.

'Oh, yes.' She frowned her chagrin. 'Well, couldn't we— Bye, Darcy,' she called out belatedly as Reed followed her from the office. 'It was lovely meeting you. I hope I see you again before I go back to the States.'

Darcy had time to lift a hand in parting to the other woman before Reed firmly closed the door behind them, his face having taken on a hunted look as his mother suggested other shopping she would like to do while she was in London.

Darcy slumped back in her chair once they had gone, knowing now that Reed would never ever see her as a woman he could desire, that with her

own single-minded forgetfulness she reminded
him too forcibly of the vague mother he
obviously adored but had no patience for! He
might pity her, but he would never desire her.

It was a stunning realisation for the woman
who loved him more than life itself, who had felt
that way about him from the first night they met.

CHAPTER TWO

WEAR your sexiest dress, Marc had told her. She didn't own any sexy dresses, although she had several she had bought to go on business trips with Reed, when acting as his hostess was often necessary; classically designed dresses that were suitable for any occasion. She had taken the black dress she wore tonight the last time they went away together, and for all the notice Reed had taken of her the material might just as well not have clung to her every curve so that the minimum of underwear could be worn beneath it.

Reed just didn't see her as a woman, only as his secretary. And she had loved him from the moment he had arrived at the office building in answer to the night security man's call that night not quite seven months ago. He had seemed amused by the mistake she had made then, had taken her out to dinner so that they could conduct the interview. After only managing to get four interviews in the two months she had been in London, and only being short-listed for one of those, she had found Reed's relaxed way of interviewing her highly enjoyable.

She had told him about her family, being her parents' only child, talked confidently of her last two jobs, her five years at the bank and the three months as a family helper to a widower and his three children, had shrugged off his surprise at the complete change of career she had made by telling him she had quickly realised it had been a mistake. He had told her how he sympathised with that, how after moving to America with his English mother, American father, two sisters and a brother at the age of ten he had been urged by his father to enter into a sporting career but had found the excitement of high finance much more to his taste. They had talked like old friends, and at the end of their meal Darcy had been so bemused by him that she had left the table wearing only one shoe! That had been when she had told him, in her embarrassment, about the dozen unmatched shoes in her wardrobe, because of her habit of slipping off her shoes while she ate and forgetting to put them both back, always feeling too embarrassed to go back to the restaurant and ask for her left shoe back! After meeting his mother today she was surprised Reed had still given her the job after she had told him that!

She knew for certain the love she felt for him would never be reciprocated.

And in the meantime there was Marc. Five years younger than Reed, at thirty, he was also much less intense; their dates were always fun and entertaining, Marc accepting the way she occasionally forgot things with a casualness that spoke of tolerant affection. She hoped it wasn't more than that, because Reed occupied all of her heart.

'Where are we going?' she asked with suspicion as Marc kept turning to grin at her as he drove.

'My apartment.'

'Your apartment!' Her eyes were wide.

'Yes,' he confirmed with relish. 'I'm going to throw you down on the bed and have my wicked way with you!'

'Marc . . .?'

'You should see your face!' He laughed at her nervousness. The open-necked brown shirt and fitted trousers he wore were casual but smart. 'You're so easy to tease,' he chuckled. 'I can assure you I don't intend having an audience the first time I make love to you.'

'Audience? But— First time you make love to me . . .?' she repeated in a squeaky voice, as the second part of his statement was absorbed.

This time he gave a shout of laughter. 'Fun to be with, too,' he told her warmly. 'After spending the day with women who take their clothes off for me as soon as they get in the door, your naïveté is totally refreshing!'

She knew that a lot of the work Marc did was for magazines and advertising, that very often it involved scantily clad women parading about his studio most of the day. In fact, the first time she had taken some papers down to Marc's studio from Reed, a model wearing only a pair of bikini briefs had answered the door! She had run back upstairs to tell Reed she thought his photographic partner was making blue movies on the side! Reed had found that very funny, accompanying her back down to the studio, to be greeted by the same model as Reed explained Marc was doing a publicity layout for the briefs. No one had explained—and she hadn't liked to ask—why the model wasn't wearing a bra!

She did know that Reed had been very friendly with the model, that he was on the same terms with a lot of the models Marc used, hence his nickname of Reed the Rake. Reed did seem to be an advocate of 'safety in numbers', dating no woman exclusively in the almost seven months Darcy had known him.

'Marc, if this is your surprise——'

'You would rather pass,' he mocked self-derisively. 'No wonder Reed finds you easy to have around; you're probably the only woman in his near vicinity that he hasn't been to bed with!'

Darcy flushed, the statement evoking her own fantasies of being in bed with Reed, fantasies that she knew would never come true. 'My relationship with Reed is purely business, you know that,' she said stiffly. 'We work well together.' Usually!

'Hey, I'm not complaining.' He punched her playfully on the chin. 'Reed would be a difficult man to follow. In fact, I don't think I'd even try!'

Not for the first time she wondered why it couldn't have been this man she fell in love with. He was so much less complicated than Reed, had a wickedly attractive sense of humour, was handsome enough to have been one of his own male models. And he took care of her with an easy familiarity she hadn't known since she left home. But all she could feel for him was liking, or the love of a friend, a good friend.

'Then why are we going to your apartment?' she persisted.

'Wait and see, birthday girl.' He drove the car into the underground car park beneath his apartment building. 'But try and look a little less like I'm kidnapping you!'

She was still badly shaken from the events of this morning, and wasn't being very good company for Marc; she forced a bright smile to her lips. Whatever Marc's surprise was, it couldn't be that bad!

At least Marc had had the decency to warn her to look her best, although after ten minutes of meeting people she barely knew Darcy decided she hated surprise parties, especially ones given for her. She had met most of the people before because she knew Marc, but even so none of them were actually good friends of hers. But Marc, at least, seemed pleased with his surprise.

'Can we expect an announcement tonight or is Marc going to wait until you get to the church before telling you about that, too?'

Darcy turned sharply at the sound of that mocking voice, forgetting the drink she held in her hand as it slopped precariously over the side of the glass, only narrowly missing the front of Reed's pale green silk shirt as he stepped back out of its way.

She swallowed hard, hadn't realised he was here until this moment. 'Your mother?' she croaked incongruously.

He swept a mocking glance over the gathering, the beautiful men and women standing around talking in relaxed groups, the drink flowing freely as loud music blared from the new stereo unit

Marc was so fond of. 'I don't think she would quite fit in here, do you?' he drawled softly, his gaze returning to her.

'No,' she acknowledged ruefully, knowing she didn't exactly 'fit in' either.

Reed frowned at the slightly lost look that had come over her face. 'If you don't stand up for yourself now, Darcy, you aren't going to stand a chance after you become his wife!'

She blinked up at him owlishly. 'I don't know what you're talking about.'

'Marc,' he said abruptly.

She glanced over to where Marc was standing, four women making up the rest of his group, all of them hanging on his every word. She shrugged. 'He's enjoying himself.'

'Darcy, he— Never mind,' he dismissed violently. 'Each to his—or her—own.'

'Marc isn't mine. And I certainly don't intend marrying him.' She shook her head. 'I don't know whatever gave you the impression I was. Marc is just a friend.'

'Like we're friends?' Reed scorned.

Colour darkened her cheeks. Until today she had believed she and Reed were at least that, although there was so much more on her side. 'No, not like we're friends,' she acknowledged. 'But——'

'I didn't think so,' he derided. 'He'll walk all over you if you give him half a chance!'

Her mouth tightened resentfully. 'That won't be anything new!' She gave a small gasp of dismay as she realised what she had said. 'I meant——'

'I know what you meant, Darcy.' He sighed heavily. 'And I realise I was rough on you earlier, but this is different. Marc is not husband material. Not for you anyway.'

'I really don't know what business it is of yours, but I have no intention of marrying him.'

'No?'

'No!'

'He isn't going to object if I whisk you off to Florida on Sunday?'

Her eyes widened. 'Florida?' She knew his family had lived in Orlando the last twenty-five years, that he occasionally visited them. But he had never taken her with him before.

'Don't look so surprised, Darcy,' he taunted. 'I do have business dealings in the States, you know.'

'I do know, but—it's a bit sudden, isn't it?' Even for him! He hadn't mentioned anything about it earlier today.

His mouth thinned, his eyes narrowed. 'Something has come up. Are you willing to come with me or not?'

'Of course I'm willing.' She frowned. 'There's nothing wrong, is there?'

'Nothing I can't handle,' he bit out in a voice that boded ill for someone.

'Reed!' Marc joined them, slapping the other man on the back in greeting. 'I know I invited you, but after your mother's arrival this morning I didn't expect to see you tonight.'

'My mother has gone to bed,' he drawled. 'And she assured me that she wanted me to go out and enjoy myself.'

'And are you?' Marc challenged, his arm about Darcy's shoulders.

Reed met that challenge. 'Not particularly. Don't you think it might have been a little—kinder, to have warned Darcy about all these people being here?'

'Then it wouldn't have been the surprise it was intended to be,' Marc scorned.

'Darcy doesn't like surprises; haven't you noticed that?' he rasped.

He made her sound about as interesting as yesterday's bath water! OK, so she liked her private life ordered and repetitious, but things were less likely to get forgotten that way! Besides, she had enough excitement in her life just being his secretary.

'She liked this one,' Marc claimed stubbornly. 'But if you aren't enjoying the party you can always leave.'

'I think I will,' Reed snapped, pulling Darcy's hand up from her side to slap a small parcel into it. 'Happy Birthday. I'll give you a call tomorrow about Sunday,' he added abruptly, striding over to the door, to be waylaid by a beautiful red-head as he pulled it open. He murmured something in her ear; the woman's throaty laugh floated in the air as they left together.

'I wonder what—or who—has upset him?' Marc mused a little dazedly, the two men usually being good friends away from the office.

'His mother,' she said wearily, slowly unwrapping the present Reed had given her.

Marc pulled a surprised face. 'She seemed rather sweet to me.'

'Reed can't stand it when someone isn't as organised as he is,' she murmured, tears filling her eyes as she looked at the gold necklace nestled in the velvet box, a gold unicorn threaded on its length. A fantasy animal for a woman who lived in a dream world sixty per cent of the time!

'Dear, are you sure you're going the right way?' Maud Hunter fretted. 'I'm sure that sign back there said——'

'Mother,' Reed interrupted patiently. 'As you always read a road map upside down because it "makes more sense", I don't think you're in a position to judge signposts!'

Maud turned to give Darcy a vague smile as she sat in the back of the Mercedes, and Darcy sighed softly as she was once again left to her silent perusal of the countryside on the way to Southampton, feeling as if Maud had made her a conspirator to her vagueness with that smile.

Reed had telephoned her early that morning and asked her if she would like to accompany them to Southampton, saying that his mother would like it if she did. Darcy had still been a little befuddled from waking up, otherwise she might have found an excuse not to come.

The party had dragged on until almost three in the morning, and as it was supposed to be for her she hadn't been able to leave until everyone else had without offending Marc, then had insisted on helping him tidy the apartment, refusing his invitation to stay the night, despite his assertion that he would sleep on the sofa. Considering the early hour of Reed's call she had a feeling he had expected either to have Marc answer the call or for her to still be at the other man's home.

She was also sure that Reed would rather she hadn't come today, despite his mother's obvious pleasure in having her here. After all, he had two of them to keep in line now!

She wished it could have been different, wished she could have been as cool and self-assured as the women who had occasionally called for him at the office. But she doubted she would ever be any different now, had trained herself too well. As long as she continued her efficiency in the office she could continue seeing Reed; she would be the one to hand in her resignation if she thought her work was below the standard he demanded. But it was going to be a long time before he forgot what had happened yesterday.

She held the unicorn aloft in the palm of her hand as it hung suspended about her neck. It was a beautiful piece of jewellery, and she knew she would always wear it simply because Reed had been the one to give it to her. But it represented how Reed felt about her, a woman who lived in a world that wasn't quite real, as the unicorn wasn't. He could have no idea how close she had come to living completely in that shadow world, how much more attractive it could look than the starkness of reality. But she never talked to anyone about that twilight world except Rupert. And she knew her secret was safe with him.

'. . . continue on, Darcy?'

She looked up guiltily as she realised Reed's mother had been talking to her, paling a little as she saw the fierce glitter in Reed's eyes as she met his gaze in the driving-mirror. It wasn't fair! Yesterday had knocked her confidence in her abilities for six! She wouldn't normally be so nervous about a little lapse in concentration.

She sat forward in the seat, giving Maud a dazzling smile. 'I'm sorry, I was miles away,' she admitted honestly, challenge in her eyes as she met the mockery in Reed's.

'I know how you feel, dear.' Maud nodded without chagrin. 'I'd forgotten just how beautiful England was,' she added wistfully. 'It's so green and—and lush.'

'And damp and cold in the winter,' her son drawled unromantically.

Maud gave him an impatient look. 'You needn't try and put me off; I have no intention of intruding on the cosy life you've made for yourself here away from the rest of the family. I was just stating that I had forgotten how lovely England is.'

Reed scowled. 'You're more than welcome to move in with me any time you want to, you know that.'

Green eyes that were so much kinder than her son's could ever be twinkled merrily at Darcy before she winked conspiratorially. 'I'd drive you to distraction in a week!' she mocked without rancour. 'Your father always said I was the reason you were such a good athlete; you were trying to run away from home!'

Darcy held back her own smile with difficulty. Although she didn't really know what she had to smile about: Maud Hunter had just confirmed what she had already guessed, that Reed would run a mile from falling in love with a woman even remotely like his mother.

'You know that isn't true——'

'I know it *is* true,' his mother chuckled, turning to Darcy. 'And I was just asking you if you would like to stop for lunch or continue on?'

She shrugged, glancing at Reed. 'Whatever the two of you would prefer.'

'Very diplomatic,' he drawled, his mouth twisted. 'Mother would like to stop, I would like to go on.'

No wonder they had asked her; now she was in the position to upset one of them. But the rumblings of her stomach told her she had missed breakfast and that it would be grateful if she didn't give lunch a miss too. 'It might be nice for your mother if we stopped for a pub lunch,' she suggested blandly. 'But, of course, if you would prefer not to bother . . .'

Maud laughed softly. 'I like your secretary, Reed,' she smiled.

'I get the feeling she likes you, too,' he muttered, looking around for a pub that served lunches.

Darcy had never seen him quite this caustic before; obviously his mother had a strange effect on him. He definitely wasn't his usual charming self.

The pub that Reed finally chose had a formal

restaurant at the back overlooking the gently flowing stream that was populated by several swans and ducks, the pub itself looking centuries old with its thatched roof and beamed ceilings. But for all the notice Reed took of its rustic charm he might have been sitting in a bus shelter! He really was in a bad humour today.

'Just ignore him, dear,' Maud advised her after they had ordered their meal. 'He's always been the same until he's eaten. Even as a baby——'

'I'm sure Darcy isn't interested in that, Mother,' he snapped impatiently.

'I wonder why it is that men don't like to admit they were ever drooling babies that needed their nappies changed just like other people?' Maud mused.

'Mother!' Reed threatened in a thunderous voice, Darcy having difficulty holding back her amusement as he shifted uncomfortably on his seat.

'Well, until you bring a nice girl home for me to tell all your childhood anecdotes to Darcy will do just fine,' his mother dismissed. 'Besides, I'm sure she *is* interested in learning you're as human as the rest of us.'

Darcy gave the older woman a sharp questioning look, blushing a little at the warm understanding she found in Maud's eyes. The other woman knew she was in love with her son!

She did enjoy hearing more about Reed's childhood, so different from her own in that the family had moved between England and America for several years before finally settling in

America, all four of the children adapting well to the move. Reed scowled all through the telling of it, but like every other woman in love Darcy loved hearing about his childhood. And if Reed were even more distant by the time they left the restaurant it couldn't be helped; she could have listened to Maud talking about him all day. And most of all she enjoyed hearing the pride in Maud's voice when she spoke of her son's achievements. She would have liked to have known Lloyd Hunter, the two men sounding very much alike, the father having given every encouragement to Reed to succeed, even though he would have preferred his son to take up the sporting career he hadn't ever been good enough to enter himself.

Once they reached Southampton docks it all became rather a rush, stopping for lunch having made them late—Darcy was sure Reed must be biting his tongue to stop himself saying 'I told you so!'—and so they barely had time to see Maud settled into her suite on the gleaming white cruise-ship before the signal for visitors to leave was sounding.

'The Mediterranean for a month.' Darcy sighed enviously as they lingered to wave goodbye to Maud as she stood up on the deck, turning to give Reed a rueful look as he made no reply. 'I know,' she grimaced, 'knowing my luck I'd probably be seasick the whole time!'

His face relaxed into a smile for the first time that day. 'If my mother can survive I'm sure you could.'

She turned away so that he shouldn't see the hurt in her eyes. 'Thank you for the necklace, by the way,' she told him woodenly, waving enthusiastically to Maud.

'I saw it in a shop window and it seemed appropriate,' he dismissed.

She nodded. 'It's lovely.'

'I thought so.' His eyes were narrowed on the paleness of her face, the intensity of his gaze causing Darcy to look away. 'Darcy?' He frowned, his hand under her chin as he tilted her face up to his. 'What's wrong?'

'Wrong?' she evaded.

'For a moment you looked——' He broke off, shrugging. 'Lost, somehow.'

She gave him an overbright smile. 'Don't you wish you were going on the cruise?' She looked up blindly to where she knew hundreds of happy faces were smiling in anticipation of the trip ahead, her inability to see them having nothing to do with not wearing her contact lenses.

'No.' A glittering hardness entered his eyes. 'I have something much more important to take care of.'

Darcy blinked up at him, frowning at his vehemence. 'In Florida?'

'Yes,' he rasped.

'What——'

'Not here,' he dismissed harshly, looking around pointedly at the other people seeing off relatives.

Maybe it was the business in Florida that was making Reed so bad-tempered even now his mother had left; he certainly still looked grim.

She tried to think of any business dealings they had had with Florida in recent months, and couldn't remember any.

'Is there any way I can help, Reed?' she offered once they were back in his car, Darcy beside him in the front this time.

'No,' he rasped.

Darcy lapsed into silence, knowing from experience that Reed would talk when he was ready, or not, whatever the case might be. More often than not he didn't feel the inclination to confide in her.

It wasn't until they were on the plane the next day that he felt 'ready' to talk, and then what he had to say first stunned her and then rocked the foundations of her being!

'Darcy?' he prompted sharply at the choking sound in her throat which was her reaction to his news.

She moistened lips gone suddenly dry. 'Could you— Would you say it again?'

'We'll be staying with my youngest sister Diane——'

'I heard that part,' she dismissed impatiently, wondering why he could possibly think she would feel in the least distressed about that.

'I want everyone, including my family, to think that I'm just on vacation——'

'I heard that bit, too.' She was breathing deeply as she waited to see if he would repeat what she had *thought* she heard him say earlier.

'Surely you aren't going to find it that difficult letting people believe we're—a couple?' he mocked.

A couple. Yes, he had definitely said it again. And he couldn't know how difficult she would find that to do; if he had he would probably put her on the first return flight to England. But he obviously didn't know, would never have suggested it if he had ever guessed she was in love with him.

'Marc never has to know about it if that's what you're worried about,' he drawled dismissively.

Marc—she hadn't given him a second thought, had no doubt that while she was away he would be dating one of the numerous models who were so available to him! It was herself she was worried about; how far did being thought 'a couple' go?

'I can understand that you're a little reluctant——'

He couldn't!

'... but just think of this as a working vacation,' he continued lightly.

Working? It would be *purgatory*!

'We don't have to act as if we can't take our hands off each other or anything like that,' he assured her. 'It should be enough if you just act unsecretaryish,' he derided. 'And I don't think you'll find that too difficult to do!'

'Now just a minute——'

'I meant, of course, that the holiday setting should make it easier for you to just relax in the Florida sunshine and enjoy yourself.'

Darcy eyed him suspiciously, not at all sure he had meant anything of the sort. She unconsciously took the unicorn in the palm of her hand and moved it from side to side on the gold chain. 'Am I to be told what all this is about?' She frowned.

'Some of it.' He nodded evasively. 'As much as I feel you need to know.'

'I don't think I like the sound of that.' She shook her head, still frowning. 'Reed, just what are you up to?'

'It isn't a question of what *I'm* up to,' he told her grimly. 'I'm the innocent one in all of this!'

'Innocent?' she repeated in a strained voice. 'If you're innocent then that must mean someone else is—guilty, of something?'

'Yes,' he rasped.

Darcy felt the rush of blood in her ears, could feel a threatening blackness descending. 'I don't think I can do this, Reed,' she denied, desperately trying to cling to consciousness.

'You don't have to do a thing.' He was too lost in his own grim thoughts to notice how pale and agitated she had become. 'Just enjoy your holiday, I'll take care of the rest.'

'What "rest"?' She swallowed hard, her fingers tightly gripping the arms of the seat.

'It's business, Darcy,' he bit out.

'What sort of business?'

'Private business,' he grated.

'Is anyone going to get hurt?' she asked shakily.

'I hope not. But I can't guarantee it,' he added, at her indrawn breath.

Not again, she couldn't go through something like that a second time!

CHAPTER THREE

'FOR God's sake, Darcy, did you forget to eat breakfast or something?' Reed demanded as he fanned her still body with the in-flight magazine.

The comical picture they made, her slumped in her seat while Reed glowered over her, would have been funny if she didn't feel so sick—and frightened. She struggled through the fog in her brain to try and remember what had given her this sense of foreboding. Then she remembered, sitting up so suddenly that Reed's face spun dizzily in front of her again.

'Here you are, Mr Hunter.' The concerned stewardess arrived at his side bearing a tray with a cup of either tea or coffee on its surface. 'Are you sure you wouldn't like me to see if there's a doctor on board?'

'No—thanks.' He took the cup and saucer. 'Darcy just needs her hourly dose of syrup!'

The fact that she took two spoonfuls of sugar in her coffee and drank the brew constantly had become a standing joke between them during the months she had worked for him, his own coffee always taken black and unsweetened, although he rarely drank it. But Darcy didn't feel much like laughing at the moment.

'I didn't forget to eat breakfast,' she snapped as the stewardess left after giving her a sympathetic smile. 'I just fainted, that's all.'

'That's all?' He thrust the coffee at her none too gently.

'Yes.'

'Why?'

She blinked her puzzlement at the narrowing of his eyes, anger boiling up in her to replace the panic that had made her faint the way that she had. She wasn't going to think about *that*, had trained her mind not to think about the blood, the— Oh, God, she *wouldn't* think about it!

'Surely a pregnancy would only enhance the story that we're "a couple"?' She used her anger at Reed to block out the painful memories.

'If you're pregnant then you shouldn't be drinking coffee!' he grated, reaching for the cup.

She deliberately took a sip of the hot brew, instantly feeling a little better. It was strange, but she really did think her metabolism needed all the glucose she poured into it. 'I'm not pregnant—— '

'You just told me you were!'

She sighed. 'Wasn't it what you were thinking?' she rasped. 'But as far as I know immaculate conception only took place once in history!'

Reed drew in a controlling breath. 'Your levity couldn't come at a worse time—— '

'Oh, I wasn't joking, Reed.' She steadily met his searching gaze.

'You're a virgin!' he said disbelievingly.

Her gaze dropped in the face of his incredulity. 'I didn't say that,' she mumbled.

'After dating Marc for six weeks I doubt you could,' he derided.

'Reed——'

'Why did you faint?' he demanded to know in a brisk voice.

She put her cup down carefully on the table in front of her. 'Reed, I don't think I can help you with whatever you have planned to do in America,' she told him softly. 'I'm no good at pretence, and—and I'm not sure I agree with what you're doing,' she added in a rush.

His eyes had narrowed. 'You don't know what I intend doing!'

'No. Well.' She shrugged. 'Whatever it is I'm sure it can't be all that nice if it has to be done in secret.'

'No, it isn't *nice* at all,' he derided. 'But then neither is poaching on my business deals.'

'But you're already so rich and successful, surely you don't need——'

'And just how long do you think I'll stay rich and successful if every deal I try to make in America is sabotaged?' he rasped grimly. 'Because that's what's happening.'

'How?' she gasped.

'My interest in certain deals is quietly being leaked to other interested parties, one party in particular, enabling them to step in and make the deal before I get the chance. And it's a nice healthy pay-off for the person leaking the information. Someone is cashing in on my knowledge—and I do mean cashing,' he grated. 'It couldn't last forever, of course; the golden goose, that's me, was bound to become suspicious eventually. But in the meantime whoever is involved in this has made themselves a nice hefty profit for no outlay but my trust.'

Darcy frowned. 'Do you have any idea who would want to do such a thing?'

'Someone who knows me well enough for me to have confided my interest in certain deals to them, someone I must trust—and someone who can be bought!'

Darcy could quite see how Reed's interest in a deal could be taken as an indication that money and success would follow; Reed had the ability to spot a good deal with no apparent effort on his part. She could also see that the person leaking that information to a competitor had to be someone really close to Reed to know of his interest.

She gave a sudden gasp of dismay. 'You don't think someone in your *family* could be involved?'

'I often talk to them about deals I'm interested in over here,' he revealed. 'But, hell, they're my family, none of them would do this to me!'

She could see that he really wasn't as sure of that as he would like to be. As an only child herself, she had no idea what it was like to grow up with two sisters and a brother all younger than yourself, although she could imagine there had been a few disputes when they got older. But surely none of them serious enough for any of them to betray Reed in this way?

'I realise I should have told you all this yesterday and then asked if you would mind posing as my girlfriend.' Reed sighed, running a weary hand across his brow. 'But I have to admit that the idea didn't occur to me until last night when I realised that I'd panic whoever is involved if I just arrived out of the blue. But I've lost three deals, three good deals, during the last six months, too many for it to be just a coincidence. I have to find out who is doing this to me, Darcy.' He looked at her with pained eyes.

'You have no idea?'

'None,' he rasped. 'But I will. With your help.'

She knew the last was a question, and now that she knew more about it she realised this bore no resemblance to what had happened two years ago, that the only hurt likely to be incurred was to Reed himself, and that would be emotional, not physical.

'I just have to sit about looking besotted by you?' She attempted to lighten the situation.

'Not too besotted.' His mouth twisted. 'Neither my brother or either of my sisters could ever really believe any woman would be besotted by me.'

Then they must all be blind—or prejudiced! Women had trouble not falling in love with Reed, from what she had observed. And as one of the women who had failed she knew what she was talking about!

'I suppose families are always like that when it comes to lovers and spouses,' she dismissed.

He grimaced. 'I have to admit, I never understood what Wade and Chris saw in my two sisters, and as for what Marie sees in Mike . . .!' He pulled a face. 'As you said, families are like that,' he acknowledged ruefully.

His family sounded as if it were very close; she could see why it was so important to know none of them would hurt him in this way. 'If I leave my contact lenses out they'll think I'm looking at you with dreamy eyes,' she joked, desperately wanting to remove the pained bewilderment from shadowed eyes.

Reed took her hand in his, studiously looking at the slender fingers with their clipped nails. 'I've been a bastard to you the last few days.' He spoke quietly. 'And I'm sorry.' He looked up at her with blazing green eyes. 'First that business with my mother, and now this; I used you as a punchbag.' He smoothed the hair back at her temple. 'You didn't deserve any of it.'

She couldn't break contact with his gaze, felt as if she were drowning in those green velvet depths; his thumbtip moved in a featherlight caress across the sensitised skin at her temple. 'Whew!' She finally managed to break away from the spell he had been casting. 'Your sisters and brother obviously don't realise how lethal your charm can be!'

To her surprise—and delight—he threw back his head and laughed, a deep throaty sound that she realised she hadn't heard in some time. 'I can't say I ever remember *trying* to charm my family,' he drawled, still smiling. 'I don't think they're charmable!'

If they weren't charmable they were certainly *charming*, Darcy found out a few hours later.

After she had agreed to help him Reed had suggested they get the connecting flight straight on to Orlando where all of the Hunter family lived, and when they arrived at his sister Diane and her husband Chris's house later that evening, it was to find the whole family had been invited over for dinner, Diane's bikini-clad body telling them it was an informal dinner party!

'Sorry.' Reed gave Darcy a grimace once Diane had told them the news. 'If you would rather give dinner a miss and go straight to bed . . .?'

She swallowed hard, nervous about meeting so many new people all at once, all of them very important to Reed. She knew that it didn't really matter that much if she made a good impression or not, but she did want them to like her. But she didn't want to meet them all looking as she did now, very dishevelled after the hours on the planes. 'If I could just freshen up first . . .?'

'Of course.' Diane nodded enthusiastically; a younger, much more volatile version of her mother, her long hair so blonde it looked silver, eyes as green as her brother's twinkling merrily as she gave Darcy a thorough, if friendly, appraisal. 'You aren't at all what we were expecting, you know.' The words seemed to flow without volition.

'Diane!'

She gave her brother a cheeky grin. 'I didn't say I didn't approve,' she told him impudently. 'I'm pleasantly surprised. The others will be, too. Linda was sure you would be bringing a bored sophisticate.'

'She should talk!' Reed derided.

Diane laughed; she had been lucky enough to

inherit her mother's fine bone structure, too, her beauty something that would never fade, only refine. 'She's trying to persuade Wade to move his office to Miami; she says she's sick of the backwoods!'

'And Wade is naturally refusing to go anywhere,' Reed guessed drily.

'He was your friend first, what do you think?' Diane mocked.

He grimaced. 'I think Linda had better get used to the idea of growing old in Orlando; Wade will never move from here.'

'Right!' His youngest sister laughed again. 'I hope you forgive me for letting the whole family invade like this.' She looked ruefully at Darcy. 'For months we all thought Reed's secretary Darcy was a man; you can imagine our surprise when Reed told us he was dating you!'

Darcy avoided looking at Reed as she sensed his disgust with the assumption his family had made concerning her sex. 'I'll forgive you anything,' she smiled limply, 'if you'll only tell me that the whole of the house is air-conditioned!' Her expression was one of desperation.

They had simply transferred from one airline to another once they had reached Miami; the airport being cool and comfortable, the heat and humidity of early May had almost knocked Darcy off her feet once they went from the airport to the car Reed had hired. On the drive from the airport to Diane Donavan's home she had convinced herself, with the benefit of the blasting air-conditioning, that she must have imagined the intensity of the humidity outside. One step outside the car had told her she hadn't imagined a thing. At this rate she was going to spend her entire stay hurrying from air-conditioned buildings to the car and back again!

'You'll get used to it,' Diane grinned.

'I don't think so.' She shook her head regretfully, the cloying heat outside, even in early evening, making her feel drained; goodness knew what it must be like during the day! And she didn't think she wanted to find out. 'Please say the whole of the house is air-conditioned!' She couldn't imagine sleeping if it weren't.

'It is.' The other woman nodded.

'Thank God.' Darcy leaned weakly against Reed.

'But I'd organised eating beside the pool.' Diane frowned. 'If you would find it too much——'

'No! No . . .' she protested half-heartedly. 'Just ignore me; as you said, I'll soon get used to it.' Never in a million years! She couldn't understand why people actually *chose* to live in this heat.

Diane didn't look convinced. 'You have your usual room, Reed,' she told her brother distractedly.

'Fine.' He took control. 'Let's go, Darcy.' He prompted her down the hallway that obviously led to the bedrooms in this beautiful bungalow.

Darcy couldn't understand how he could look so cool when he was still wearing the dark grey suit and neatly buttoned shirt! She had taken her jacket off the moment they had left the airport, had rolled back the sleeves to her blouse, and she had still felt hot and uncomfortable.

'I'm sorry,' she groaned. 'Your sister is going to think I'm a complainer.'

'She won't think anything of the sort,' he dismissed easily, opening the door to the bedroom that bore an obviously male stamp.

It was a beautiful house, long and low, set among numerous trees, the lake visible a short distance away, several other houses set among the trees in the same way. The décor she had glimpsed on entering the house continued into the bedroom, elegant but comfortable; Diane and Chris Donavan were obviously as wealthy as Reed.

'Don't worry.' Darcy pulled a face as she sat down on the side of the double bed. 'I'm not about to ask where my bedroom is, or where you're going to sleep tonight,' she derided.

His eyes were narrowed as he slowly straightened from placing their cases side by side on the floor. 'You knew Diane would expect you to share a room with me,' he realised slowly.

She was glad he hadn't said 'sleep together', because she felt sure Diane didn't expect them to *sleep* at all! That young lady had had a definite speculative gleam in her eyes when she told Reed he had his usual room. And why not? Reed had probably been a teenager the last time he hadn't slept with the women he was dating, and that was almost twenty years ago.

'It hadn't occurred to you,' she realised with

some amusement, knowing he was totally disconcerted at the idea of them sharing a bedroom. Disconcerted didn't begin to describe the way she felt!

'No, it hadn't.' He sat down on the bed beside her, frowning heavily. 'What do we do now?'

'You aren't very flattering, Reed,' she laughed, trying to hide the pain she felt at his aversion to the idea of sharing this room with her.

'This is serious, damn it,' he scowled. 'Acting like we're on holiday together is one thing; *this*,' he looked round at the double bed they both sat on, 'is something else.'

'Afraid Samantha will mind?' she taunted, alluding to one of the women he was dating in London.

'I hadn't given her a thought.' His cold dismissal couldn't be doubted. 'It was you I was worried about.'

He needn't worry about her, she would be begging to share this room with him in a moment! Couldn't the man see that she was in love with him? His sister had seen it at a glance, a gleam of approval in the eyes that were so like Reed's.

She shrugged. 'We could always move to a hotel.'

Reed was shaking his head to that idea before she had even finished the suggestion. 'Diane would never forgive me. God, nothing like this occurred to me,' he breathed heavily.

And now that it had he obviously didn't like it! Darcy stood up. 'It's a big bed, Reed,' she dismissed with a casualness she was far from feeling. 'I doubt we would even have to touch if we didn't want to.'

'The problem is,' Reed stood up to pace the room, 'will we want to?'

Darcy turned to give him a sharp look, blinking her surprise as Reed seemed to be looking at her for the first time as if she were a moderately attractive woman. He had to choose now, when her hair was in even tighter curls than usual, her make-up was non-existent, her clothes creased from the hours of travelling, and she was so tired her body knew it was really one o'clock in the morning and not the eight o'clock the bedside clock insisted it was!

'Neither of us is stupid enough to believe that platonic garbage,' he frowned. 'When a man and woman get into bed together, body chemistry takes over.'

Be still my beating heart, she cautioned shakily. 'We could always ask Diane if she has a room with single beds,' she suggested breathlessly. 'Tell her I'm a very restless sleeper.'

'That wouldn't work,' Reed frowned. 'After all, I'm supposed to be in love with— Watch out!' he cried as Darcy took a step backwards and overbalanced over the suitcases. He managed to catch her before she hit the carpeted floor. 'Don't tell me,' he drawled indulgently. 'You forgot they were there!'

She forgot *everything* as he held her against him. She had never realised before, but he had gold flecks in his eyes, those specks seeming to burst into flames as their gazes remained locked. Darcy could feel a constriction in her chest, her breasts barely moving against him as she was afraid even to breathe lest she broke the spell, his eyes searching hers now, the warmth of his breath touching her mouth as his face seemed to be moving closer. Or perhaps she had been the one to move up to meet him, she didn't know. And she didn't care, craving the touch of the warm hardness of his mouth on hers.

'I've brought you both—whoops!' drawled an amused female voice that wasn't Diane's. 'Maybe you should lock the door or put up a "Do Not Disturb" notice when you're—occupied, Reed?' the woman added derisively.

Irritation at the interruption, and then anger, darkened his eyes as he put Darcy firmly away from him before turning to face his elder sister. 'Maybe if you had knocked, Linda,' he grated, taking the two glasses of what looked like iced lemonade from her hands, the obvious reason for her intrusion.

In colouring, the two Hunter sisters were very similar, Linda also possessing that beautiful silver-blonde hair, although the silken tresses were confined in a smooth chignon on this elegant woman, and her eyes, rather than being green, were more of a turquoise colour, clear and sparkling as the Aegean Sea. But where Diane was short and slender, this woman was almost as tall as Reed, the perfection of her curves clearly visible in the turquoise bikini she wore. Another difference between the two women was the expression in their eyes; Diane's had been warm and friendly, this woman's were cool and questioning.

It would be interesting meeting the men who had married these two vastly differing women!

But if she had been looking at Linda O'Neal, then the other woman had been returning that perusal, the same surprise that Diane had shown reflected here in even greater quantity.

'I know,' Darcy decided to put an end to the silence that had fallen over the room, 'I'm not what you were expecting. But I am a definite improvement on a man, I hope!' Her candid gaze dared the other woman to say the 'only just' that seemed to be hovering on her painted lips!

To Darcy's surprise amusement softened the turquoise eyes. 'If you can stand up to Reed like that——'

'Oh she can—and does,' he drawled, sipping the lemonade as he enjoyed the exchange.

'Then I think you're a definite improvement on what I was expecting!' Linda gave a slow smile of welcome. 'Now could you save your lovemaking until later,' she drawled with a return of the arrogance that was so like Reed's. 'The steaks are almost cooked, and you know how upset Diane gets if anyone delays her barbecues.'

Heady perfume lingered in the air as she left as suddenly as she had arrived, and Darcy turned to look at Reed with raised eyebrows.

He grimaced. 'Maybe we should have stopped over in Orlando after all. Meeting the whole family *en masse* like this when we're tired from travelling and they aren't hardly seems fair.'

She grinned. 'I think we're holding up very well.'

'Tell me if you still feel that way once you've met Mike, too!'

Mike Hunter proved to be a younger version of Reed, with none of his arrogance. And on closer inspection he had blue eyes, not green.

Talking of closer inspections, the whole family seemed to be giving her one! Reed had suggested that, as they were late, and the pool was readily available, they might as well forgo the showers they had intended taking and change straight into swimwear, offering her the use of the bedroom while he went into the adjoining bathroom. She hadn't realised when she threw the bikini in her suitcase in England that it would bear the brunt of so much critical appraisal only minutes after her arrival in Orlando!

Diane was helping a red-haired giant of a man with laughing blue eyes and a cheeky grin as he cooked steaks over the barbecue; Linda was on a lounger next to a tall, dark-haired man with serious dark eyes; and a woman, who she guessed had to be Mike's wife, sat on the edge of the pool with her feet dangling in the water, her black hair gleaming ebony as she turned around, sensing the sudden interest in the newcomers, her advanced pregnancy becoming obvious as she did so. And then there was Mike Hunter, proving to be just as devastatingly formed in the black swimming trunks as Reed had when he had emerged from

the bathroom minutes ago. Although of similar
height and build to his brother, the younger man
seemed to have none of Reed's reserve. In fact,
far from it!

'Welcome to Florida.' He kissed her familiarly
on the mouth. 'The state of oranges, Disney
World, and the occasional forest fire raging out of
control.'

'And the Hunters,' the red-haired giant
murmured mockingly.

'Don't be put off,' Mike grinned. 'We're not a
bad lot really. Come on, I'll introduce you to
everyone.'

'Reed . . .?' She turned to him appealingly as
Mike dragged her off; he shrugged his shoulders
defeatedly.

'Don't worry, you're safe with me,' Mike
assured her suggestively.

The woman sitting at the pool's edge laughed
at Darcy's slightly dazed expression. 'You are
safe, Darcy, because Mike knows I'd punch him
out if he did more than look.'

Mike looked sheepish at the taunting rebuke
from the tiny dark-haired woman. 'It's hell being
a prospective father!' he confided woefully.

Marie only laughed again. She was obviously
of Italian descent, one or two generations
removed. Darcy decided she liked her.

In fact she liked all of the Hunter family, from
the flirtatious Mike, the pretty Marie, the
beautiful Diane, and the sophisticated Linda, to
the quietly spoken man with the dark hair, and
the man with the red hair who looked as if he

didn't take anything in life seriously. It was the latter two that surprised her; the red-haired giant cooking the steaks turned out to be Linda's lawyer husband, Wade O'Neal, and the man with the serious dark eyes was Chris Donavan, Diane's hotel-owner husband. She would have put them the other way round. Still, they said opposites attracted. Maybe there was hope for her and Reed yet!

She certainly couldn't believe any of his family was involved in leaking those business deals. Three of the people here were his siblings, the other two men good friends of his; only Marie seemed to be in the least an outsider. And she refused to believe that Reed's heavily pregnant sister-in-law could be responsible.

No wonder Reed was so bewildered.

CHAPTER FOUR

'COME on, let's go for a swim.' Reed grabbed hold of her hand, his own momentum having her running at his side in seconds, the two of them hitting the water together.

The shock of the water's coldness sent her fighting back towards the surface, blinking to clear her vision, water cascading over her face.

Reed surfaced several feet away, swimming lazily across the pool to join her. 'I'm sorry,' he frowned as he watched her shake the water from her hair, 'I forgot all about your contact lenses.'

'*You* forgot?' she teased, treading water at his side.

'*Touché*,' he drawled. 'Did you lose your contacts?'

'Didn't you know?' She grinned, feeling a hundred per cent better now that she was in the cool water. 'You can do anything in them!'

Dark brows rose over mocking eyes. 'Anything?'

'So they tell me.'

'Don't you know?'

'Well, not about everything, no,' she teased. 'But give me time.'

'Feeling better now?' he prompted abruptly. 'You looked as if you were about to collapse from the strain a few minutes ago,' he explained, at her questioning look.

Her humour faded as she glanced across to where his family were talking and laughing together as they prepared dinner. 'It wasn't because of the heat. I——'

Suddenly he was very close, his legs brushing against hers as they moved together in the water. 'I know it distresses you that it might be one of the family that's involved in this,' he frowned. 'But I just want you to enjoy yourself and let me deal with that.'

'But——' Her concerned protest was abruptly halted by the descent of his mouth on to hers, and Darcy felt dizzy all over again, her lids fluttering closed, her body betraying her as it curved warmly into Reed's, her arms moving silkily about his neck. The kiss changed, became exploratory, searching, demanding, as Darcy sighed her satisfaction at being in his arms at last.

'You two seem to be living on love instead of food,' Linda drawled from the side of the pool. 'But if you want to eat tonight you had better get out; dinner is definitely served!'

'Leave them alone, Linda,' Mike complained. 'I was enjoying the floor show.'

'Pervert!' Diane rebuked good-naturedly.

'Not at all,' her younger brother refuted. 'There was something very pure about that kiss.'

'Pure?' Wade scorned. 'They——'

Darcy couldn't seem to tear her gaze away from Reed's, locked in the warm sensuality that had engulfed them, the emotion seeming to have taken Reed completely by surprise. But not Darcy. She had always known that if ever Reed were to take her in his arms she would meld in to him. She had been proved correct, had felt like the other half of him.

'Reed,' Diane prompted impatiently. 'You and Darcy are the guests of honour!'

'Does that mean the rest of us were an afterthought?' Mike mused without rancour.

'It means you all invited yourselves,' Diane returned. 'Reed——'

'Leave them alone, honey.' Her husband spoke quietly. 'Can't you see they're in love?'

Darcy saw by the sudden wariness in Reed's eyes that he had heard that last remark at least— and he hadn't liked it. He should have been pleased; at least his family were convinced of their relationship. But he looked far from pleased as he swam to the side of the pool, levering himself out on to the side before turning to hold out a hand to assist her from the water. He released her as soon as he was politely able to do so.

'Did you have a chance to meet Mom before she went on her cruise?' Diane asked as they all sat around the pool with plates of steak, baked potato, and salad.

'Darcy drove down to the boat with us,' Reed answered for her.

'Great, isn't she?' Wade grinned, not looking in the least as Darcy expected a lawyer to look. And not seeming at all the sophisticated man she would have expected Linda to marry, the quietly reserved Chris seeming more her type than this big bluff man.

'You didn't say that the day she muddled the gears on your car and drove straight through the garage doors,' his wife taunted drily.

Wade grimaced at the reminder. 'OK, so she's a great mother-in-law at a distance.' He shrugged.

'Oh, and what about the time she——'

'Darcy isn't interested in hearing all about Mother's "accidents",' said Reed, cutting in on his brother abruptly.

'*You* wouldn't be here if she didn't have those accidents,' Diane bubbled. 'She muddled up her dates and thought she would be safe.'

'Diane!' Reed frowned at her.

She returned that frown, obviously taken aback by his sharpness. 'You know, you've changed since you moved back to England.'

That was because, even if he had once been able to talk teasingly with his family about his mother's absent-mindedness, he no longer found it funny when he was discovering he had a secretary almost as bad!

Reed shrugged. 'I'm sorry.'

Diane flushed uncomfortably. 'No, I am. I was so pleased when you rang to say you were coming over and now I'm arguing with you.'

'We should have let you and Darcy have at least one evening alone before descending on you,' Mike acknowledged ruefully. 'I suppose we were all curious.'

'About Darcy,' Reed drawled knowingly.

Mike gave an inclination of his head. 'When my dedicatedly single brother telephoned to say he was bringing a girl home, I'm afraid you couldn't keep any of us away!'

'I noticed,' Reed grimaced, regret darkening his eyes as he met Darcy's gaze. 'You didn't think meeting all of you like this might put Darcy off?'

'Hey, we aren't that bad,' Wade protested.

'You're worse!' Reed amended indulgently, relaxing slightly. 'It's like walking into a scene from the Waltons!'

'And which part do you play?' Linda drawled. 'Pa?'

'Over you lot?' Reed returned without rancour. 'Never! But you have to admit Darcy has the hair and freckles to play Elizabeth!'

Darcy felt very self-conscious as they all turned to look at the riotous red curls covering her head, even tighter than they usually were as they were allowed to dry naturally after her swim. As for the freckles, they could never be doubted!

She was familiar with the television programme about the large Walton family set during the nineteen-thirties and forties, and she didn't think she liked being compared to the carrot-haired girl with the sinus problem that played the part of the youngest member of the family.

'The programme never seemed to be the same to me after John-Boy grew a foot from one series to the next!' she said drily, alluding to the fact that the first actor to play the oldest son in the series had decided to leave and his replacement had topped him by at least a foot—even if he did have the original man's blond hair and mole on his cheek!

'That's an American institution you're maligning,' Chris derided mockingly.

Darcy smiled at him shyly, feeling a little as if she had an affinity with him, both of them less extrovert than the rest of the family. 'I like the programme, I just——'

'Uh uh,' Mike shook his head. 'You can't back down now,' he said with relish.

'I wasn't trying to——'

'We may never recover from this crushing blow,' he continued in a wounded voice.

'Pipe down, Mike,' his wife scorned. 'You only watched the programme twice!'

'Who wants to watch a programme about a houseful of children when you grew up in one! Even Chris and Wade were always at the house before you two married them!' he told his sisters disgustedly.

'College friends of mine,' Reed supplied, as Darcy looked puzzled.

'I think you're very wise not to have told her too much about us, Reed,' Linda mused. 'She probably *would* have been put off.'

'There's no might have about it,' Marie derided. 'I almost was.'

'But my fatal charm proved to be irresistible,' Mike leered.

'If you're referring to the fact that you carried me off to bed a week after we met and refused to let me out until I married you then I suppose you could call it that,' Marie said drily. 'But if you're talking about our first date when you took me to a baseball game, forget it!'

'She loves me really,' Mike confided in Darcy.

'It was either marry you or die of starvation,' his wife maintained derisively.

Darcy was fascinated by the affection this whole family seemed to have for each other, if slightly overwhelmed by it. Whenever she went home her parents showed their steady quiet love for her, but as only children themselves, too, their family was a small one.

She could feel the situation starting to slip away from her, the automatic defence mechanism that had become so much part of her life the last two years, whenever things became too much for her, blocking out her surroundings and the light-hearted banter continuing between the Hunter family as she stared sightlessly at the glittering pool.

'I think I'll take Darcy for a walk around the lake.' Reed's softly spoken words penetrated her world of silence. 'Darcy?' he prompted.

She looked at him vaguely. 'Lovely.' She stood up, the clatter of china as it hit the ground telling her what she had done. Her dinner plate had been resting on her knees and she had stood up without giving it a second thought. 'I'm so sorry.' She hastily bent to pick up the plate and the pieces of food that had been on it, her face bright red as she looked up to see Reed holding out the knife and fork to her. 'I'm so sorry,' she told Diane again as her concerned hostess came over.

'Don't be silly,' Diane dismissed lightly. 'There's no harm done.'

Maybe not to the plate, but to Reed finally

seeing her as a woman there was; she had just reminded him that she could become so absent-minded she forgot there was a plate balanced on her lap. No one *forgot* they had a plate on their knees! But she just had.

'Maybe I *should* have warned you about them,' Reed frowned as they strolled over to the lake's edge. 'I'm overwhelmed by them sometimes, so God knows what they do to people who don't know them!' He gave a rueful grimace.

'You're overwhelmed?' Darcy echoed dis-believingly.

He shrugged, giving her a sideways glance. 'After you've been away from them for a while they can seem like a blanket, warm and comfortable at first, and then it becomes suffocating. Do I sound ungrateful?' He frown-ingly quirked dark brows.

'Probably like most older brothers in a family of four,' she teased. 'It must be quite a responsibility.'

His brow cleared a little as he looked at her admiringly. 'That's very astute of you; no one else has ever realised that's exactly how I feel at times. It was part of the reason I made the break away ten years ago. Diane and Mike, even Linda most of the time, are quite happy to stay in the close family circle. I decided I wanted more from life than that.'

'Did you get it?'

'No.' He gave a self-derisive snort. 'I still worry about all of them, even though I'm over four thousand miles away!'

'But you've always seemed like such a loner.'

'Until something like this happens,' he acknowledged grimly. 'That's when I feel like putting my head down and pulling the blanket around me until it's all over.'

This was a side of Reed she had never seen before, the less than confident Reed, the mere man beneath all the power and money. She liked him all the more for showing her this side of himself, *loved* him all the more.

He stared out across the lake, the deep red setting of the sun having left a beautiful pink haze in the sky. But the beauty of it was lost on Reed, as his next words confirmed. 'Pulling that blanket around me wouldn't do a damned bit of good this time,' he rasped. 'Not when there's a damned great hole in it!'

The placing of her hand on his arm was wholly instinctive. 'Reed——'

'Let's not talk about that any more now, Darcy.' His arms were pure muscle about her waist as he pulled her up into him, their warm flesh seeming to sizzle into one as her slender height melded with his power, heat of a different kind coursing through them as he slowly lowered his head. 'Don't forget, we're the floor show!' he muttered savagely.

If only the touch of his mouth on hers had matched his tone and manner she might have had some small chance of resisting the onslaught, but as he kissed her with slow, languorous passion she stood no chance! Floor show or not, she stood on tiptoe to return the caress, her arms curved sensuously about his neck as she allowed herself

the luxury of entangling her fingers in the curling
dark hair at his nape.

With the slight pressure of her hands in his
hair his mouth hardened on hers, plunging them
both deeper into the heated glow that threatened
to burn out of control—and take both of them
with it. Reed *couldn't* manufacture this response,
the hardness of his arousal pressed against her
stomach, just to convince his family of their
intimate relationship!

'Reed!' She gasped for sanity as his hand
closed possessively over her breast, the instant
hardening of her nipple against his palm giving
the lie to her protest. But she wasn't about to give
an X-rated display to his family.

Reed looked at her dazedly for several seconds,
and then a cold remoteness glazed his eyes. 'You
see,' he rasped. 'Body chemistry takes over. I
have to talk to Diane about tonight's sleeping
arrangements!'

'Reed!'

His eyes were narrowed as he turned to her,
looking completely unapproachable.

'Not in front of all your family, *please*,' she
groaned, embarrassed colour in her cheeks.

'You would rather they continued to think
we're lovers?' he derided.

Darcy walked past him, her head held high. 'I
don't want them to think we aren't!'

Reed chuckled softly as he fell into step beside
her. 'You're right, Diane would be on the
telephone to Linda and Mike first thing in the
morning if we asked for separate bedrooms.'

'And would you enjoy seeing me humiliated in that way?'

His mouth tightened at the quiet query. 'I'll think of something,' he finally grated.

'Good—because I'm definitely not sleeping in the same bed as you!'

She had been tempted; God, how she had been tempted. But to hear that flesh-quivering, bone-dissolving, skin-tingling desire she had felt in his arms reduced to 'chemistry' had been enough to show her she would be making a mistake to believe it would mean any more than that to Reed. Chemistry. Huh!

'Reed is throwing us all out.' Mike softly interrupted her thoughts as she made her way back to the house some way behind Reed. 'He says the two of you are tired and he doesn't want us partying while you're both trying to sleep. If I were him I'd forget all about the sleep,' he added teasingly.

Darcy looked over at the patio where Reed seemed to be organising the departure of his family with all the finesse of a drill sergeant! 'I'm sorry.' She gave Mike an embarassed smile. 'I'm so tired I'm sure you wouldn't disturb me if you all stayed.'

Mike looked at her with warm eyes. 'No, Reed is right—we should never have all come here like this tonight. But Reed bringing a girl home was too unusual to miss.'

'And you all wanted to take a look at me in case I disappeared as suddenly as I arrived!'

'Something like that,' he grinned. 'We've been

debating for years about what sort of woman he would eventually fall in love with——'

'I'm sure none of you guessed it would be someone like me!' she mocked.

'None of us thought he had this much sense!'

Sense? This boisterously close family could really imagine Reed would fall in love with someone like her! 'We aren't serious about each other——'

'Reed is always serious,' Mike cut in broodingly. 'Deadly serious.'

'Maybe about his work——'

'About all things that matter to him,' his brother corrected. 'We've missed him here the last few years.'

Darcy looked at him frowningly, seeing only sincerity in the clear blue eyes. Reed appeared to be the anchor this family needed to stop it floating away. A family had to separate, go its own way, grow, but inevitably a close family like this one would drift back together again; Reed had been fighting that since his move back to London. Seeing him here with his sisters and his brother, she was sure he needed them as much as they needed him, that his enforced solitude would soon be at an end. None of his family wanted to live in his pocket, but it was important for them to know he was close if they needed him. Or he needed them. Reed seemed to have omitted to realise it was a two-way need.

'Marie is ready to stop your golfing trips for a month if you don't stop flirting,' Reed drawled as they joined the rest of the family.

Mike pulled a suitably chastened expression. 'Anything but the golf!' He put a hand up to his heart as if he had been mortally wounded.

'I don't think that was the right answer, Mike,' Reed drawled at Marie's disgusted snort.

His brother groaned, his moment of seriousness seconds earlier as he spoke to Darcy completely erased. 'My other pleasure in life is getting virtually impossible.' He looked pointedly at his wife's rounded body.

'Michael Hunter!'

'I didn't say I disliked the situation,' he placated his wife as they walked down the driveway to their car, opening the door for her with a flourish. 'It's just that golf is my only physical outlet now.' He winked at the people standing in the driveway as he closed the door on Marie's reply.

'We had better be going too, Wade,' Linda drawled once Mike and Marie had driven away. 'Reed's obviously sick of the sight of all of us already!'

'I don't blame him for wanting to be alone with Darcy.' Her husband put his arm lightly about her shoulders. 'I remember a time when *you* couldn't wait to get home!'

Darcy looked at the couple sharply as she sensed the underlying bitterness behind Wade's remark. Obviously things weren't as cosy as they appeared in the O'Neal household.

'That was before you couldn't wait to get *out* of it,' Linda returned in brittle tones, getting in behind the wheel of the black and gold Trans

Am, the engine roaring into life as she waited only long enough for Wade to fold his long length in beside her before accelerating away.

'What the hell was all that about?' Reed frowned darkly.

'Linda and Wade have fallen out, that's all,' Diane dismissed, the smile she gave not quite reaching her eyes. 'It happens in the best of marriages.'

'Yours?' Reed looked at her with narrowed eyes.

'Heavens, no.' Diane's rebuttal was genuinely scornful, her arm draped through the crook of her husband's. 'Chris and I are very happy together.'

Reed stared after the tail-lights of the Trans Am. 'Surely the trouble between Linda and Wade can't just be her desire to move to Miami?'

'Who knows. Leave them alone to work it out, Reed,' Diane encouraged, pulling him back into the house. 'They will, you know.'

'Do they argue a lot?'

'I told you, all married couples do. Now let's see about transferring your luggage to another bedroom,' she organised briskly.

Darcy and Reed's move to a room with two single beds instead of the tempting double was done with the minimum of fuss—and no questions asked.

'What did you tell them?' Darcy asked awkwardly as she lay in the bed across from Reed's, the blush in her cheeks evidence that she had been completely aware of his nakedness as he slipped off the robe and climbed into bed—her own bedclothes pulled up to her chin. Of all the things she could have forgotten to pack it had to have been her nightgowns!

Reed shrugged uninterestedly. 'That it didn't bother me but that you always prefer to sleep alone this time of the month.'

'You didn't!' she gasped.

He looked at her with puzzled eyes. 'Why not?'

She put her hands up to her suddenly burning cheeks. 'Oh, Reed!' she groaned her embarrassment.

'Honey, every woman of child-bearing age has them,' he reasoned softly.

'Yes, but——'

'It was all I could think of at the time; could you have thought of anything better?'

'No. But——'

'What do you think is really wrong between Linda and Wade?' he asked suddenly.

Both of them were naked beneath the sheets, they had just been calmly discussing one of woman's more delicate bodily functions, and he wanted to talk about the problem between his sister and her husband!

But they were here to discover who was betraying his confidences, and any friction between members of his family had to be suspect. Darcy just wished it could be different, and she knew Reed was hoping it would be someone outside the family that was responsible—even if the possibility were very remote. He wasn't a man who told just *anyone* of his business interests.

'It's probably nothing important, as Diane said,' she dismissed.

'She didn't say that.' He shook his head. 'She said they would work it out. That seems to imply that they always have in the past. That doesn't sound like a happy marriage to me.'

'Reed, Wade was your friend long before he married Linda,' she reasoned.

'He's also my lawyer over here,' he revealed abruptly. 'I wonder if a price can be put on friendship?' His thoughts were distracted as he settled down on to the pillows, one arm flung back behind his head.

Darcy heard him sigh several minutes later, having come up with no reply to the pained question. She glanced at him. His eyes were closed, his chest moving steadily up and down in deep sleep.

So much for chemistry!

CHAPTER FIVE

'HE said he had to go and see some old friends.'
Diane grimaced at her across the breakfast table. 'I
thought the two of you were on vacation together.'

'We are.' Darcy smiled tightly, having woken
up to find the bed across from hers empty, his
sister telling her he had breakfasted and gone out
over an hour ago. She realised that these 'old
friends' of Reed's were probably people who
could tell him what was going on over here, but
that didn't make his just leaving her here to cope
any easier to accept.

'You mustn't mind him,' Diane encouraged
indulgently. 'He hasn't been home in such a long
time.'

'I really don't mind,' she dismissed.

'That's good.' Diane nodded her relief. 'Now,
are you sure I can't get you some pancakes or
waffles to go with that coffee and toast?'

Her stomach did a somersault just at the
thought of them after the terrible night she had
just spent, lying awake long after Reed, only half
sleeping then as she tried to maintain a hold on
the bedclothes. She would have to do something
about getting a nightgown today!

'I hope last night didn't tire you too much,' the
other woman said, watching her as she stifled
another yawn behind her hand. 'Once Linda and

Mike decide to do something, nothing will stop them.'

'I enjoyed meeting them all. Really,' she reassured firmly as Diane still looked doubtful.

'Reed wasn't too happy about the situation,' Diane grimaced.

'I'm sure you misunderstood him. Did he happen to say when he would be back?' She sipped her coffee with a nonchalance she was far from feeling. While she liked Diane, and was fairly sure the two of them were going to get on together, she was always a little shy with new people, didn't make friends all that easily. Reed could at least have asked her if she would like to go with him this morning instead of just leaving her to the tender mercies of his sister.

'Before lunch,' Diane shrugged. 'If that's any help,' she added.

It was only ten o'clock now, and that could mean any time until one o'clock!

'Did you know Reed before you became his secretary?' Diane sat down opposite her.

She had been expecting this friendly curiosity— and dreading it. Damn Reed! 'No,' she answered unhelpfully—and then felt guilty as she saw the disappointment in the other woman's eyes. 'I met him for the first time when I went for the interview. I—We realised a short time ago that we were attracted to each other,' she invented.

'Is it—serious, between the two of you?' Diane asked with feigned casualness.

Darcy's mouth quirked. 'You mean, are my intentions towards your brother honourable?'

'Jeez, did I sound that bad?' Diane winced. 'I must be out of practice.'

'I gather Reed hasn't brought many women home by the reaction his family has had to me?'

'Now who's being obvious?' Diane laughed softly.

She grimaced. 'Why don't we just tell each other what we want to know and save ourselves a lot of time?' she agreed.

By the time Darcy had finished her breakfast and helped Diane clear away she had learnt that Reed had never introduced one of his women to his family before, hence the uncontained excitement about her arrival. She knew she had disappointed Diane by informing her that she and Reed had only a casual relationship, that they were just taking a holiday together while Reed visited his family.

'Are you sure that's the way Reed feels too?' Diane frowned.

She nodded. 'We've just been having a good time together, keeping it light.'

'I thought—We *all* thought—Did he give you that necklace?' the other woman probed interestedly.

Darcy gave her a puzzled look, surprised at the change of subject. 'Yes. But——' She picked up the unicorn in her palm, glancing down at it as she saw the gleam of satisfaction in Diane's eyes at her answer. 'It was a birthday present,' she revealed slowly.

'It's lovely,' the other woman acknowledged lightly.

'Diane?'

'Yes?'

That feigned innocence was making her wary.
'Diane, what——'

'As we have a few hours before Reed gets back,
would you like to go shopping?' Diane interrupted
briskly. 'There's a really good mall at Altemore
Springs. About twenty minutes' drive away.'

Darcy could tell that the subject of the necklace
was closed, for now at least, and she did have to
buy herself a nightgown before tonight. Besides,
shopping would kill a little time, and that had to
be better than sitting around the house with
Diane, getting herself even more deeply entangled
with the lies about her relationship with Reed.

'Reed is very worried about your sister and her
husband,' she ventured casually on the drive.

Diane pulled a face. 'Linda and Wade are
always arguing. Wade's a corporate lawyer, and
very serious when it comes to his job, but when
he gets home he likes to relax, have fun. Linda is
one for appearances. It doesn't make for complete
harmony, I'm afraid,' she shrugged.

'It's nothing—deeper, than that?'

Diane didn't seem to resent the personal
questions from a relative stranger. 'They've been
married for six years now, I think Wade wants to
have a family of their own. He doesn't have any
family of his own left, and I think he wants to
father a few O'Neals.'

'But Linda doesn't want children?'

'Not yet, no.' She sighed. 'I think Wade has
issued an ultimatum.'

Darcy frowned at that. 'Having children when you don't really want them can't be the answer.'

'I'm sure Wade knows that,' Diane said with certainty. 'He's just trying to shock Linda out of what amounts to plain stubbornness now. Marie's pregnancy isn't helping the situation.'

'Marie and Mike seem very happy.'

'They are,' Diane confirmed, driving the large car with ease. 'Mike has a lot on his mind right now with the stagnation of property speculation, but I'm sure they'll muddle through. I'm just glad Chris got out when he did.'

'Got out?' she prompted softly, feeling a little guilty about the ease with which she was extracting information about the family from Reed's sister. But it had to be better than Reed asking himself.

'He and Mike were in partnership together for a while.' The other woman shrugged. 'Until Chris saw the hotel and decided to buy and run that instead. It's one of the most exclusive in the area,' she added proudly. 'Of course, tourism is down a little the last couple of years because of the strength of the dollar, but we're still doing very well.'

That was obvious from the house and the way the couple lived. But it was also obvious that all of the family had their problems, Wade feeling some resentment towards the Hunters because Linda seemed quite satisfied with them as her family instead of having children of her own; Mike, and consequently Marie, having monetary problems; Diane and Chris feeling a tightening of their purse strings, too. But none of those things seemed enough for any of them to want to obtain money at Reed's expense. Although Reed didn't seem to realise his family had any problems.

He frowned heavily later that night when she told him what she had learnt from Diane, the two of them once again lying in the beds across from each other, Darcy more comfortable this evening in the loose cotton nightshirt she had acquired on their shopping trip this morning, the material not even remotely see-through; she had checked that before buying it!

Reed had walked about naked for several minutes before getting into bed, as if he expected her to be used to unclothed men in her bedroom. Even if she had been, she was sure she would still have been affected by the lithe beauty of his body, looking like the statue of Apollo she had once admired. Except he was very much a flesh and blood man.

They had dined alone with the Donavans this evening. Chris was a little more outgoing when not in a crowd, although the bubbly Diane still monopolised much of the conversation, and the three of them were happy to let her do so, Reed being in a taciturn mood since his return from his visit to 'friends'. Darcy relaxed by the pool before going for a swim; she had been wrong about the heat, she was starting to enjoy it.

'I can't really blame Wade for wanting a family; I'd be getting a little impatient myself by now,' Reed finally grated. 'But, hell, I can't believe that would be enough for him to let me down in this way!'

Neither could Darcy. 'He only wants a family, Reed. That doesn't seem to be enough reason to fraudulently obtain money at your expense. There has to be more to it than that.' She shook her head. 'Didn't you find out anything today?'

He sighed. 'The people actually making the deals aren't talking, obviously, and no one else seems to know that anything strange is going on.' He scowled. 'In fact I'm being given the impression I'm imagining things!'

'Are you?'

'No.'

He looked grim, and Darcy couldn't blame him for feeling the way that he did. He loved all of his family, and the strain of thinking one of them was involved in this was starting to show. She decided it was time to take his mind off his problems for a few minutes.

'Diane seemed very interested in the unicorn necklace you gave me,' she mentioned casually, watching for his reaction.

One brow rose slightly. 'Oh?'

She could sense the tension in him even though it wasn't physically noticeable, just a feeling she had, his eyes staying an emotionless green. 'Why do you think that was?'

He shrugged, looking indifferent. 'I have no idea. Maybe she just liked it.'

'She guessed you had given it to me before I told her you had,' Darcy persisted.

'Lovers often give each other jewellery,' he dismissed.

'Reed——'

'Look, could we go to sleep now?' He turned to her with blazing eyes, the glow from the bedside lamp between them giving an ebony sheen to the curly hair on his chest that disappeared in a V towards his thighs, a sheet resting lightly over his hips. 'It's late and I've been up since dawn.'

'Couldn't you sleep?' Her eyes widened.

'That damned sheet kept slipping off you all night,' he rasped impatiently, unrelenting in the face of her embarrassment at this disclosure. 'I now know you have a birthmark on your——'

'Reed . . .!'

He gave a sudden grin, looking years younger, his eyes gleaming mockingly across the short distance between the two beds. 'It's just where your silken legs meet the rest of your body,' he added with satisfaction. 'And it isn't visible when you wear a bikini,' he drawled.

'I know that.' She was sure the colour of her cheeks matched the red of her hair. She had been so sure she had clung on to the sheet all night! But Reed couldn't have seen her birthmark any other way.

'The shape of a half-moon,' he murmured musingly. 'You would have been burnt as a witch in the old days; they didn't take kindly to red-haired women with the mark of night on their body!'

'Or green-eyed men with hair as black as the devil!' she instantly returned.

He smiled, his face bathed in warm light. 'Shall I put a warlock spell on you?'

He already had! All this talk of witches and

warlocks, and that birthmark on her thigh, wasn't doing a thing for her equilibrium. The sheet had slipped off him, too, last night, and she hadn't been able to draw her gaze away from the muscled contours of his body, knowing that he would be formidable when he was aroused. Why couldn't he let that 'chemistry' take over? She certainly wouldn't mind!

'Are you going to be able to go back to working for me after this?'

He was scowling when her startled gaze met his. 'This?' she repeated in a puzzled voice.

'Yes, *this*.' He looked around pointedly at the bedroom they shared.

She chewed on her inner lip. It probably would be difficult going back to just being employer and secretary, their relationship possessing an air of intimacy now that wasn't all pretence. But she couldn't imagine *not* working for him, seeing him every day.

'I'm sure I can,' she replied briskly. 'After all, we're only sharing the room.'

'Is that all?'

Sexual tension crackled in the air between them, Darcy's eyes widening as she saw the look of sleepy passion in Reed's eyes. She swallowed hard. 'Chemistry?'

He drew in a ragged breath. 'You're more than just passably attractive, Darcy,' he told her huskily. 'And I'm finding I have a desire for freckles. They're all over your body——'

'It's the heat,' she explained awkwardly.

'I don't care what it is,' Reed rasped. 'I want to

kiss every one of them!'

She made a choking sound as her breath seemed caught in her throat and started to cough, hastily averting her gaze as Reed got out of bed to come over and tap her on the back. 'I'm all right now.' She pushed his hand away, looking up at him uncertainly. 'Did you mean it?'

'Of course I meant it,' he sat down beside her on the bed, smoothing back the hair at her temple. 'I've always thought it.'

She was mesmerised by the liquid emotion in his eyes, held captive by those stormy depths. 'Always, Reed?' She suddenly realised the implication of what he had said. 'But——'

'Not now, Darcy,' he uttered with a groan. 'I've tried to stay away from you, in fact I've been amazed at my own success in keeping my hands off you. But you look so damned sexy in that nightshirt——'

'Sexy? *Me?*'

Reed's expression darkened. 'Whoever he was, he was a bastard,' he grated. 'You——'

Darcy had stiffened. 'Whoever who was? Reed, what do you mean?'

'The man who had you so screwed up in knots when you first came to work for me you were afraid to let anyone near you!'

Her gaze dropped away. 'I don't know what you mean,' she abruptly evaded.

'Darcy?' He tilted her chin so that she looked at him, her eyes blue lakes of pain. 'Hell,' he grated harshly. 'He's still there in your eyes!' He stood up to turn away. 'You seemed to be

different lately, and I—Oh, hell!' He pulled on
his denims, their snug fit revealing that he wore
nothing beneath.

'Where are you going?' Darcy came up on her
knees to watch him as he strode to the door.

'Out of here,' he rasped. 'It doesn't really
matter where!'

She slowly sank back down on to the pillows
once he had gone. There had been a man, Reed
was right about that, but she had let him love her
for all the wrong reasons, had let him hurt her . . .
But to explain about Jason she would have to tell
Reed everything, and she couldn't do it.

One mistake, that at the time she hadn't even
thought of as being one, and it had ruined and
governed the rest of her life. Would it never change?

'Come on, lazy, we're going out today,' mocked
that familiar voice as her nose was gently
tweaked.

Reed. And he didn't seem angry any more. She
opened her eyes as she smelt coffee.

Reed sat on the side of her bed, a cup of coffee
in his hand. 'I thought this might wake you,' he
grinned. 'I'm sure you're addicted!'

Darcy eyed him warily as she drank the hot
brew. He hadn't returned here last night by the
time she fell asleep, but wherever he had spent
the night it seemed to have agreed with him; he
looked rested and relaxed. And she felt a wreck!
It just wasn't fair the way a man never looked as
bad as a woman, even in the morning, after a
supposedly disturbed night.

'Reed——'

'Chemistry, Darcy,' he cut in self-derisively, his hand gentle against her cheek. 'I'm finding this platonic proximity a bit of a strain.'

'Is that all it is?' She frowned at the explanation. 'Last night——'

'Bringing you here was a mistake.' He stood up, his hands thrust into the pockets of his denims. 'This situation between us was a mistake,' he added grimly. 'If only I'd realised everyone would expect us to sleep together!' This last seemed to be added almost to himself.

Darcy turned to put her cup down on the side table so that he shouldn't see her wince of pain at the way he didn't even try to pretend he had found last night anything but a mistake of the moment, that close proximity with a vulnerable woman proved too much for this highly sensual man. She didn't like being thought of as a convenience, or Reed 'finding he had a desire for freckles'.

'Maybe I should go back to London——'

'No!'

'But——'

'I need you here, Darcy.' His expression was remote. 'I know I'm being ungrateful, I just— I'm sorry, Darcy. Stay,' he encouraged softly.

She would walk barefoot through a pit of snakes if he asked her to! But she wasn't sure staying on here wasn't going to be even more lethal.

'Please, Darcy.'

How could any woman resist him when he

asked so intensely? The fact that many women hadn't even tried to resist him, and on a completely different level, was ignored as she slowly nodded her head. 'All right, Reed.'

An emotion flared in darkened green eyes, too fleeting to be analysed before it disappeared as Reed smiled. 'I'll get you breakfast before we leave,' he offered. 'Diane went to the hotel with Chris today as I told her we would probably be going out,' he said, explaining the reason for his sister's absence.

'I can get my own breakfast,' Darcy protested. 'I only want toast.'

'And coffee,' Reed teased.

'And coffee,' she acknowledged ruefully.

He hesitated at the door. 'Feel like a drive today?'

'I don't mind,' she shrugged.

'As we're supposed to be on vacation I thought we could play tourist today,' he said derisively. 'Busch Gardens is just over an hour's drive away. Unless you would prefer Disney World and Epcot?'

'Which is the quietest?'

'Busch Gardens,' he answered without hesitation. 'But we don't have to go to either if you would prefer to stay here——'

'Oh no, I want to go out,' she told him eagerly. 'I've never been on an expenses paid holiday before.'

'What makes you think I'm paying your expenses? Only joking, Darcy,' he teased as she suddenly realised he had never said he was.

'Getting paid for having my complete attention; what more could any woman ask for?'

What indeed? Reed may have meant the remark as a joke, but it was all too true for her; what more *could* she ask for?

And Reed seemed determined to please her, too, with a cooked breakfast for them both on the table by the time she had showered and dressed in the pale yellow cotton top and matching shorts that were what Reed had assured her would be appropriate wear for the day.

'I think my appetite just took a different turn.' He looked at her admiringly. 'For such a little thing you have the most incredibly long legs,' he murmured, his gaze warm.

All the better to chase you with, she felt like returning, but managed to stop herself. It seemed to be OK for him to flirt with her, in fact he was enjoying himself, but she didn't think he would appreciate her doing the same to him. 'Breakfast looks lovely,' she smiled, sitting down at the table.

'Your button is undone.' Reed reached across to the large button on one shoulder of the loose blouse, his fingers lingering on the silken flesh beneath. 'You look lovely, Darcy,' he told her gruffly. 'Like a sunflower.'

'Thanks—I think,' she added uncertainly. Were sunflowers lovely? They were certainly bright, but surely a little gaudy?

He squeezed her shoulder before fastening the button with deft movements. 'Don't think, eat your breakfast,' he advised. 'You're going to need it!'

It was a warning that proved to be all too true. Busch Gardens turned out to be anything but the sedate gardens with walks down tree-sheltered pathways that she had been expecting. Also called The Dark Continent, it was exactly that, in miniature. After going through the entrance they walked into what could have been part of Morocco, with its street merchants, snake charmers and belly dancers. Darcy had to drag Reed away from watching the latter!

It was all there, hundreds of wild animals roaming free as the steam-train chugged through their midst, even yellow and white Bengal tigers in the Congo area. It was hard to believe they were still in Florida!

It was a fun day, a day completely out of time as she and Reed joined in with all the other people enjoying themselves, Darcy laughing uproariously at Reed as they went on the raft down the Congo River rapids and he managed to get soaked from head to toe before they were half way down them, her laughter turning to a shocked scream as one of the jets of water stopping them from crashing into the side caught her full in the face and upper body.

'The wet-look definitely looks better on you than it does on me,' Reed murmured mockingly as he gazed unashamedly at the pointed thrust of her breasts against the clinging cotton material.

Darcy wasn't so sure of that once they had got off the raft and the full effect of his wet clothing could be seen, his denims clinging snugly to his hips and thighs, his shirt transparent, the dark hair on his chest clearly visible. She could barely drag her gaze away, longing to run her hands——

'Thoughts like those aren't fit for present company,' said Reed, looking pointedly at the children milling about them.

Delicate colour darkened her cheeks. 'Neither was what you were thinking a few minutes ago,' she returned primly.

His mouth quirked. 'How do you know what I was thinking?'

She glared at him. 'You—Oh my goodness, my contact lens just popped out!' She closed her eyes in disbelief. The day had been going so well, too!

'Don't move,' Reed advised forcefully. 'I think I see it.'

Darcy's lids flew up as she felt his fingertips against her breast. 'Reed——'

'Found it!' he exclaimed triumphantly.

'You did?' Her breath seemed to be constricted in her throat as she felt his fingers moving against her blouse, the flesh beneath springing into life, the hardened nipples pushing against the material.

'Don't just stand there looking at it, Darcy,' Reed muttered as he held the contact lens out to her on the end of his finger, the two of them receiving several curious looks as people questioned the motives for Reed to be fondling her breast in such a public place. 'Put the damned thing back in so we can get out of here and go have some dinner,' he scowled fiercely.

'Maybe I should keep you around all the time, Reed,' she teased as she deftly used the small mirror from her bag to put back the contact lens. 'These things have a habit of popping out when you least expect them to.'

'Was that an offer?'

She looked at him sharply. Had it been an offer? Her breasts still tingled with an un-accustomed warmth from his touch, but she had meant to avert the tension there had suddenly been between them, not make it worse. And she really wasn't in the mood for another one of his hurtful rejections. Besides, there had been Jason. Reed would never understand about him.

'If it takes you this long to try and think of an answer then I guess it couldn't have been,' Reed dismissed lightly, taking hold of her arm as they slowly made their way back to the exit. 'Formal dinner or hamburger?' he asked once they arrived back at the car.

'Hamburger,' she answered instantly, having become addicted to American hamburgers on a previous trip to New York with Reed.

He smiled, as if he had already known what her answer would be.

Darcy enjoyed her meal, having worked up quite an appetite after hours of walking, looking up after dabbing delicately at the mayonnaise on her chin to find Reed watching her with amused eyes. 'At least I didn't have two, like some people did!' she defended.

He held up his hands defensively. 'Did I say anything?'

'You didn't need to.' She preceded him from the restaurant as he held the door open for her,

NOW THAT THE DOOR IS OPEN...
Peel off the bouquet and send it on the postpaid order card to receive:

4 FREE BOOKS!
An attractive burgundy umbrella—FREE!
And a mystery gift as an EXTRA BONUS!
PLUS

MONEY-SAVING HOME DELIVERY!
Once you receive your 4 FREE books and gifts, you'll be able to open your door to more great romance reading month after month. Enjoy the convenience of previewing eight brand-new books every month delivered right to your home months before they appear in stores. Each book is yours for only $1.95—30¢ less than the retail price.

SPECIAL EXTRAS—FREE!
You'll get our free monthly newsletter, *Heart to Heart*—the indispensable insider's look at our most popular writers and their upcoming novels. You'll also get additional free gifts from time to time as a token of our appreciation for being a home subscriber.

NO-RISK GUARANTEE
- There's no obligation to buy—and the free books and gifts are yours to keep forever.
- You pay the lowest price possible and receive books months before they appear in stores.
- You may end your subscription anytime—just write and let us know.

RETURN THE POSTPAID ORDER CARD TODAY AND OPEN YOUR DOOR TO THESE 4 EXCITING, LOVE-FILLED NOVELS. THEY ARE YOURS ABSOLUTELY FREE, ALONG WITH YOUR FOLDING UMBRELLA AND MYSTERY GIFT.

Business Reply Mail

No Postage Stamp Necessary if Mailed in Canada

Postage will be paid by

Harlequin Reader Service

P.O. Box 609,
Fort Erie, Ontario
L2A 9Z9

Canada Post
Postes Canada
708

PLACE THE BOUQUET ON THIS CARD. FILL IT OUT AND MAIL TODAY!

feeling a surge of excitement through her body as his arm dropped casually about her shoulders.

'You know, it——'

'I don't want any trouble, just hand over your cash!'

Reed's fingers dug into Darcy's shoulder at the harsh instruction; Darcy had frozen at the first sound of the threatening voice, finding herself looking at a youth with a gun in his pocket—pointed at them!

Reed straightened slowly. 'Now look,' he began in a reasoning tone.

'Give him the money, Reed!' Darcy bit out forcefully, the words dragged from deep inside her.

He gave her a frowning look, concern darkening his eyes at the rigidity of her body, stark fear in her eyes. 'Honey, it's all right——'

How could he say anything was all right when there was a youth pointing a gun at them! 'Reed, give him the money,' she choked shakily. 'Just give him what he wants!' Her voice rose hysterically.

'Darcy——'

'*Reed!*' She almost screeched his name at the top of her lungs.

'I said I didn't want any trouble, lady.' The youth, probably no more than twenty or so, looked around them nervously; the car park was empty of people but themselves. 'You heard her,' he taunted Reed. 'Just give me your cash and I'll go away.'

'Darcy, he probably doesn't even have a gun——'

'Would you like me to prove that?' The youth made a threatening gesture.

'*Reed!*' She was shaking so badly now she was having difficulty standing up, knew she was going to collapse, her fascinated gaze fixed on the pocket that held the gun. If he should shoot——! 'Here,' she pulled her own purse out of her bag and threw the whole thing to the surprised youth. 'Now please, *please* go away!'

He seemed satisfied with the amount of dollars padding out the purse, running over to the motorbike parked a short distance away after throwing the empty purse on the ground, and accelerating away at top speed.

Reed still looked stunned by the way Darcy had taken the initiative.

But all Darcy could see was the gun in the man's pocket, as memories of another gun, the coldness of the steel pointing at her, flooded her mind.

She could hear the scream, see the blood, feel the blackness, before she fell.

CHAPTER SIX

'MOM telephoned this after——' Diane broke off her chatter as Reed all but carried the numbed Darcy into the house. 'What happened?' she demanded to know in a calm voice.

'We were robbed,' Reed grated. 'He had a gun. Darcy—well you can see for yourself!' he said worriedly as the woman in his arms gave a shudder at the mention of the gun.

Darcy knew what they were thinking, knew they thought she was practically comatose, even though her gaze was fixed fearfully ahead. But she knew what was happening around her even if she no longer had any control over it, docilely allowing Reed to take her into the lounge and put her on the sofa. Within seconds he was holding a glass of brandy up to her lips. She shook her head wordlessly; it didn't help, she knew that from experience. She had tried it all in the past, drink and pills, but nothing blocked out the shock and horror of what had happened.

'She's in shock.' Reed turned to his sister from his kneeling position in front of Darcy. 'I think we should call your doctor——'

'No,' Darcy cut in dully.

He turned back to her sharply; it was the first word she had spoken since she had begged the youth to go away. 'God, Darcy, I've been so worried about you.' He cupped one side of her face with a gentle hand. 'Sweetheart——'

'I was so frightened,' she shuddered again.

'I know you were,' he soothed. 'Honey, you have to put it out of your mind——'

'Rupert told me it was the law of averages,' she continued as if he hadn't interrupted. 'It couldn't happen to me again he said.' Her eyes were unfocused. 'But he was wrong, so very wrong——'

'Darcy, what are you saying?' Reed gripped her shoulders. 'Have you been robbed like this before, is that why you were so determined to give him the money?'

'I told them I couldn't leave the house any more.' She spoke again as if she hadn't heard him—as indeed she hadn't. 'Rupert said the chances of it happening again were so remote as to be non-existent,' she repeated shrilly.

'I'll go and call the doctor, Reed,' Diane spoke quietly. 'I think you should put her into bed.'

Darcy felt herself being lifted, her head flopping against Reed's shoulders as he carried her through to the bedroom, too weak to do anything but let him take control. She sat on the side of the bed while he undressed her and lay her beneath the bedclothes, her hand held limply in his as she stared up at the ceiling.

But she didn't see the wood panels above her; she could only see the calloused hand jerking as the shot was fired, the roaring sound simultaneous with the movement, the woman's body falling, falling, to lie in a pool of blood. God, the blood——!

She began to scream, not even knowing she was doing it, the hysterical sobbing seeming as if it came from far away.

'It's all right, Darcy, it's only me,' Reed assured her as she stirred panic-stricken in his arms.

She began to tremble as the memory of that afternoon's horror came back to her.

'I have you safe, Darcy,' Reed soothed softly as he felt her panic increase.

Where were they? In bed. But it certainly wasn't one of the single beds she had previously occupied. Yet the room was familiar as she looked at the masculine furniture bathed in the glow given off by the small bedside lamp. It was the room she and Reed were originally to have occupied, the two of them sharing the double bed.

And it was night outside.

'The doctor sedated you, Darcy.' Reed seemed to guess her thoughts, still maintaining his hold of her. 'How do you feel now?'

Like she had two years ago, as if someone had hit her in the chest with a battering ram! The terror today when that boy had pointed that gun at them had been ten times worse, though, because this time she knew exactly the destruction the gun could do.

'Forget I asked that,' Reed rasped self-impatiently. 'Go back to sleep, love. If you feel up to it in the morning we can talk then.'

'No.' She spoke for the first time, knowing she had to tell Reed at least part of what had happened two years ago, that she owed him that much at least after today. 'I'll tell you now. I—I may not be able to in the morning,' she admitted shakily. 'And—and I think you have a right to know.'

'Whenever you're ready,' he prompted as she couldn't seem to find the right words to start.

She was never ready to recall that time. But Reed deserved some sort of explanation. 'He came into the bank just——'

'It was the bank that was robbed?' Reed was incredulous. 'I thought——'

'I know what you thought, Reed,' she said dully. 'After all, bank robberies belong to the old West, or to the larger banks with more of a cash flow. Not to a provincial bank in a little town most people haven't heard of! We had just opened when this man came in with a gun. I saw him, and I raised the alarm. I—He realised what I'd done, panicked, and started shooting.'

'You were hit?' Reed gasped in a hushed voice, his arms steely.

'Not me.' She shook her head, her eyes squeezed tightly shut as the tears silently fell. 'It was the woman standing next to me. I'd worked with her for four years, ever since her youngest child went to school—she had three, and——'

'Oh, my God, Darcy,' Reed gathered her close against him, shuddering in reaction to what she had told him. 'I never would have guessed it was something like this. How goddamn awful for you!'

'Because I raised the alarm a man was left

widowed and three children motherless,' she stated flatly.

'You did what you thought best at the time.'

'It was only money, Reed, just a lot of paper, and Jayne died.'

'Honey, he could have fired even if you hadn't raised the alarm——'

'He could have done,' she nodded jerkily. 'But he may not have done.'

'You've been blaming yourself ever since it happened,' Reed realised softly.

'Wouldn't you have felt the same?' she said bitterly. 'I haven't always been so single-mindedly vague, you know. After Jayne died I had a breakdown, complete and oh, so peaceful. It was a little like that blanket you spoke of, Reed, warm and comforting, nothing could touch me in that world. Rupert was the one to show me it was also stifling me, destroying me.'

'Rupert?' he prompted gently.

'My psychiatrist. He taught me that I have to take one day at a time, one thing at a time.'

'For a moment I thought—— Then there was no man in your past, it was this all the time?' His eyes were narrowed.

'There was a man, too,' she told him abruptly. 'It was a mistake. I thought I could cope with it, but I couldn't. That was when I decided I had to move to London, to get away from the memories.'

'And you came to work for me,' he realised. 'Darcy, you could have confided in me, I would have tried to help you.'

She looked up at him for the first time since she had begun talking, turning away again as she saw the pity in his eyes. 'Don't feel sorry for me, Reed,' she rasped. 'I was the one that lived.'

'Thank God!' His arms tightened as he buried his face in her hair.

'I'm sorry if I made you feel less than a man earlier.' She spoke against his shoulder. 'I just wanted him to take the money and go.'

'I never feel less than a man around you, Darcy,' he told her with warm emotion. 'I never could and I never will. And I know how difficult it's been for you to tell me all this.'

'Yes.'

'Do you think you could sleep now?'

Strangely enough she felt as if she could. The years had dulled the horror if not the memory of the way Jayne had died, and sharing it with Reed somehow made it easier to bear. She had never thought she would be able to confide in him about it, but now she was so glad that she had. She had never doubted that he would be supportive, he was that type of man, but now she felt a special bond with him, and she was sure he felt it, too.

'Good.' He smiled at her as she yawned, settling her more comfortably on his shoulder as he lay back. 'I'll be here if you need me.'

She had never imagined she would be able to calmly fall asleep in Reed's arms, but that was exactly what she turned over and did!

Reed didn't leave her side the next day, the two of them spending the time beside Diane and

Chris's pool, the previous day not alluded to by either of them.

Darcy had never felt so cared for as the two of them prepared lunch together, Diane having once again gone to the hotel with Chris, this time to give the two of them time alone together, Darcy felt sure.

She still felt a little weak when she thought of the second robbery, but the shock was starting to fade under Reed's warmth and caring. It was as if she were seeing yet another side of him today, all his barriers down as he concentrated on her. She had never felt so cosseted.

'Reed, isn't there something else you would rather be doing?' she asked him late in the afternoon when he hadn't left her side for a moment.

'Now that's a leading question.' He was sprawled out on the lounger beside her, both of them in swimming attire.

She blushed. 'I meant, shouldn't you be— meeting old business acquaintances?'

He pushed his sunglasses up into his hair, his eyes instantly narrowing in the bright sunshine. 'Forget all about that, Darcy,' he said harshly. 'I'll sort that out some other time.'

'But——'

'I would never have involved you by bringing you here if I'd known what you went through!' he ground out.

'How could you have known?' she sighed. 'It's a one in a million thing, we both know that. Armed robberies aren't made on the same person every day of the week!'

'It's happened to you,' he grated. 'And the thought of you in danger twists me up inside!'

'I'm fine now. Rupert said——'

'I'd like to talk to this Rupert; do you have his telephone number with you?'

Her eyes widened. 'He's my psychiatrist, Reed——'

'I know exactly who he is.' He nodded abruptly.

She swallowed hard. 'A lot of people have need of a psychiatrist nowadays, Reed. I'm not insane.'

He spun round into a sitting position, his feet placed firmly on the ground, reaching out to take her hands in his. 'I know you aren't crazy,' he rebuked gently. 'I just wanted to ask Rupert if there's anything else I should be doing to help you.'

Tears misted her eyes at his thoughtfulness. Too many people backed off or looked at her strangely once they found out she had had a breakdown and still visited her psychiatrist. She had guessed Reed wouldn't be one of that type, and yet his request to speak to Rupert had unnerved her for a minute. She should have known better!

As for his helping her any more, just being with him, cared for by him, was enough.

'Nothing else.' She smiled at him tremulously.

'I feel so damned helpless!' he burst out intensely.

And feeling helpless wasn't an emotion Reed was comfortable with, a man who liked to be in control of the situation at all times. She had known a different sort of helplessness both two years ago and yesterday, could sympathise with his frustrated anger.

'Did you go to the police about yesterday?' she prompted huskily.

He frowned and nodded. 'I called them and told them what happened. I gave them a full description of the boy. Not that it will do a lot of good. Florida has become a damned playground, and along with that have come the people who want to steal from you. I'll reimburse the money you lost.'

'The money wasn't important.' She shook her head dismissively.

'You were working for me when it happened——'

'I was spending an enjoyable day with a man I——' She broke off, her confusion evident at the way she avoided his searching gaze. Oh, God!

' "With a man you . . ."?' Reed prompted, as she had known he would.

'Like and respect,' she substituted for the admission she had been about to make. 'It was only a few dollars, Reed,' she dismissed determinedly. 'And if you try to reimburse me I'll——'

'Yes?' he prompted again softly.

'I'm not frightened of you, Reed Hunter!'

'I should hope you aren't,' he said huskily. 'You aren't frightened of this either!'

'This' proved to be the lowering of his body on to hers as she lay full length on the lounger, her head slightly elevated, Reed leaning on his elbows at her sides, his thighs pressing intimately into hers, the tips of her breasts beneath the bikini lightly touching his chest, the gossamer-like caress hardening her nipples to throbbing need.

'Are you, Darcy?' Reed murmured against her throat.

'Not with you,' she acknowledged, arching her neck to receive the moist probe of his mouth, its gentle softness sending quivers of delight down her arched spine.

'With other men?' He looked down at her with darkened eyes.

She didn't want to talk about Jason now. 'There is no other man,' she dismissed. 'Reed——'

'What about Marc?' he grated.

'Reed, *please*!' She was burning for the touch of his mouth, on fire for the mindless, totally sensual passion only he could give her. 'Please,' her voice broke on the pleading sob.

'God, when you say it like that——!' His mouth fused with hers, their bodies melding into one.

It was always like this when he kissed her; she forgot everything and everyone, thought only of Reed and the erotic love-dance his mouth made with hers.

The hardness of his body pushed against her at the same moment as his tongue glided between her lips, possessing her slowly, rhythmically, his lower body moving slightly in the same pulsating motion.

'Draw me into you, Darcy,' he pleaded as he nudged her legs apart to lie more snugly against her, his mouth returning to hers.

She felt on fire as she drew his tongue into her mouth, the hard shaft of him rubbing against the sensitivity of her womanhood, the heat spreading through her body until it threatened to rage into an inferno.

'Reed,' she gasped. 'Oh, Reed!'

His eyes were dark with passion. 'Wrap your legs around me, Darcy. Pull me into you!'

He would be deeply inside her now if it weren't for the thin layer of material between them, and she longed to have him nestled snugly sheathed inside her, the muscles contracting in her lower stomach as she moved against him in that need.

Her bikini top disappeared on to the ground, Reed's head dark against her as he bent to suckle one throbbingly rosy nipple into his mouth, his tongue a mere whisper across the fiery tip that hardened so obediently to the command, Darcy gasping at the warm rush of emotion between her thighs as he suckled her fully into his mouth in a rhythm that made her arch against him at every moist caress.

She wanted to touch him, too, could feel the hardness of him that constantly stirred against her, wanted to touch the silken sheath, to take him in her hands and——.

'God, that feels so *good*!' Reed shuddered above her.

Without her realising what she had done her

actions had closely matched her thoughts, Reed supporting himself on his elbow as her hand encircled him beneath the black material of his swim-trunks. He felt hard and throbbing, and yet his skin was silky soft to the touch, a sensual caress as she slowly began to move her hand.

'Oh, Darcy, I want——'

'Hi, I'm home!' Diane shouted from the house. 'Are you out by the pool? Reed? Darcy?'

Reed was breathing shakily, his hands shaking slightly as he gently cupped Darcy's face. 'I've been telling my mother for years that I should have been an only child, but I never wished it more than I do at this moment!' He kissed her lingeringly on the mouth. 'You have the most incredible hands——!' He groaned his frustration before levering up and diving straight into the pool.

Darcy was just refastening her bikini top when Diane came out of the house, both women watching Reed in the pool as he surfaced before striking out with long powerful strokes.

Darcy smiled at Diane, avoiding the speculation in the other woman's eyes. Reed was gliding through the water with all the ease of a torpedo that had just been launched, and a gentle survey of her mouth with the tip of her tongue had shown her lips to be tender and slightly swollen from their impassioned kisses!

'Had a good day?' she asked Reed's sister politely.

'Not bad,' Diane answered distractedly, watching Reed for several more seconds before turning back to Darcy. 'How are you feeling now?'

'Better, thank you,' she answered sincerely. 'Reed and I have just spent a relaxing day by the pool.'

'He looks relaxed,' Diane shot a derisive glance at her brother as he began yet another lap of the pool. 'I'll go and get us all an iced drink. Maybe it will help cool Reed down inside as well as out!'

Diane remained amused by what she had guessed to be her brother's sexual frustration, Reed muttering that she had done it on purpose as he and Darcy changed to have dinner with the rest of the family later that evening. Darcy knew exactly how he felt; she wanted to be alone with him, too.

But that proved to be impossible as the family once again gathered around the pool for a barbecue, Darcy finding herself sitting beside Linda, Reed helping to cook this evening.

'Diane told us what happened yesterday; I hope you're feeling better now,' Linda questioned.

'Much, thank you,' she nodded, wishing everyone would just forget about yesterday. 'The doctor said it was just shock,' she dismissed, Diane's doctor having returned this morning and declared her well again.

'It must have been awful for you,' Linda sympathised. 'I hope it hasn't put you off our country.'

'Not at all.' She hadn't doubted that Reed would have explained only as much as he had to to his family about yesterday, that he would keep her confidence about the reason she had reacted so extremely.

'You aren't safe anywhere nowadays,' Linda said disgustedly.

'It's the same in England now,' she nodded.

'I—I want to apologise about the other night.' The turquoise eyes avoided contact with Darcy's. 'Wade and I have always made it a rule never to involve the family in our arguments; you must have thought us very rude.'

'You didn't really argue,' Darcy excused lightly.

'You should have seen us once we got home!' Linda grimaced. 'Wade's pretty amiable most of the time, but he does have a temper to match his red hair!'

'Arguments often help clear the air.'

'Not this time,' the other woman sighed. 'Why is it men feel the urge to procreate?'

Darcy smiled. 'I'm sure it isn't just a male urge!'

Linda's smile was one of self-derision. 'Then I wonder what's wrong with me?'

'There's nothing wrong with you,' Darcy protested lightly. 'You just need more time.'

'But will I get it?' The other woman watched her husband as he laughed with relaxed ease as he and Reed cooked the steaks.

Darcy wished she were able to offer some words of help to Reed's older sister, but what advice could she offer about marriage and babies!

'Don't take on the problems of my family,' Reed advised as he sat down beside her after dinner, gently taking her hand in his. 'That's my job. I saw the way you looked earlier after talking to Linda,' he explained at her frowning look.

'She's so unhappy.'

He nodded. 'So is Wade. But he's promised to talk the problem through again with Linda when they get home.'

She had thought the two men were engaged only in light banter, but it seemed Reed had found the opportunity to talk to his old friend about more serious matters. 'Linda seems very determined,' she grimaced.

'I know my sister well enough to know that it's her stubbornness that's half the problem now.' He sighed impatiently. 'She's great with kids, would make a great mother, and —Hell, they'll work it out, Darcy,' he dismissed suddenly. 'Without any help from you or I. You, young lady, are going to be too busy helping me work out my problem to concern yourself with theirs.'

Her eyes widened. '*You* have a problem?'

Reed placed her hand on his thigh over the black shorts he was wearing with a green T-shirt, the evidence of his arousal was warm against her. 'Finishing what you started,' he muttered.

'What *I* started?' she repeated with mock indignation, her face glowing.

His eyes were dark with desire. 'Darcy, I need to have you touch me like that again.' His fingers curved her hand hard against him. 'Do you understand?'

How could she doubt the conclusion he wanted their earlier caresses to take? How could *he* doubt that it was what she wanted too?

She moistened her lips. 'Isn't it a little early to go to bed? Your family will think it very odd, this sudden need to drag me off to bed.'

'I'm only interested in what *we* think,' he grated with a return of his usual arrogance. 'And we aren't going to bed—yet.' He stood up before she could answer. 'Darcy and I are taking over the jacuzzi,' he announced to his family in a voice that didn't allow for questions or offer any explanations.

'Don't mind us,' Mike couldn't resist taunting.

'We won't,' Reed returned warningly.

Darcy felt shy as she climbed into the water next to Reed, his shorts and T-shirt and her wrap-around skirt discarded on to a chair, the two of them sitting under the water.

They were across the garden area from the rest of the family, the high sides of the jacuzzi giving them total privacy, the slightly warmed water whirling about them at the press of a button. Darcy could feel her body relaxed by the soothing pressure of the water, putting her head back with a sigh of satisfaction. This was totally decadent—and she loved it!

'Nice?'

'Very,' she murmured, feeling as if every pore in her body were open—for Reed.

She opened her eyes wide at the gentle caress of Reed's hand up her leg to her inner thigh. 'Are you sure these things are legal?' she gasped breathlessly, her legs instantly parting for him.

'Jacuzzis?' he murmured against her cheek. 'Oh, they're legal. But what we're about to do in one may not be!'

'It might also be impossible,' she teased.

'Want to bet?' he challenged softly.

As the water swirled and foamed about them Darcy gave herself up to the magic of his kiss, her arms curved about his neck as she moved her mouth joyously against his.

'Tonight I'm going to kiss every one of those freckles,' Reed promised gruffly. 'And that beautiful mark of the half-moon, and——'

'Don't talk, Reed.' She encouraged his mouth back to hers. 'Just do it!'

'Yes, ma'am!' He smiled his satisfaction at her aggression.

'Women can be frustrated too, you know,' she defended irritably. 'Forget I said that; of course you know,' she frowned. 'Just don't expect me to have the experience of your other women, Reed,' she warned self-consciously. 'My one relationship was very—limited.'

'I'm glad.' He touched her mouth with gentle fingertips. 'It may be chauvinistic and totally unfair of me, but I don't think I could bear it if I knew another man had loved you as thoroughly as I'm going to.'

It had to be different with Reed, because she loved him in a way she never had Jason. She had gone to Jason for all the wrong reasons, she would give herself to Reed for all the right ones!

She looked confidently into passionate green depths. 'Make love with me, Reed.'

His throat moved convulsively. 'I've imagined this moment,' he groaned.

'Reed——'

He moved in the water to lie between her thighs, Darcy gasping as she realised he had removed her bikini bottom and his swimming trunks as they talked, their thighs entangling as he pressed that silken length of himself against the flowering bud of her womanhood.

He paled suddenly, his breathing constricted. 'We have to get out of here,' he gasped in a pained voice.

'Reed?' She voiced her uncertainty as to what was wrong.

'This hasn't happened to me since I was in high school,' he rasped through gritted teeth, pulling on the black trunks in jerky movements. 'Darcy, I was going to kiss and caress you out here until we were wild for each other, until we could make our escape and go to the bedroom and finish this, but if I don't get out of here and take you to bed now I'm going to disgrace myself and then neither of us will have any pleasure for some time. Do you understand what I'm saying?' he grated, pulling her bikini briefs on with difficulty.

It wasn't funny, she knew it wasn't, and yet after her disastrous encounter with Jason the thought of Reed, strong invincible Reed, losing complete control in the way he described over *her* brought a mischievous twinkle to her eyes.

'You wouldn't be so amused if that happened, Darcy.' He scowled irritably as he helped her out of the water. 'I'm not one of these sexual athletes all those women's magazines are supposed to rave about; I only do one gala performance a night!

And maybe an encore in the morning,' he added self-derisively.

No matter how disgruntled it made him she couldn't help laughing softly as they walked back to the house. Despite her love for Reed she had felt some trepidation about their lovemaking, but that had completely disappeared in the face of Reed's discomfort at his complete lack of control. She felt elated by the admission, completely confident in her ability to satisfy him.

'That was quick,' Chris drawled.

Darcy gasped back a laugh at the unintended double edge to the words, determinedly keeping her face averted as Reed told his family she was tired and he was taking her to bed.

'You can laugh now, you little devil,' Reed groaned after dragging her into the house, the bedroom door closed behind them.

She couldn't help it, she did exactly that, too amused by the situation to control the bubble of laughter.

'And when you've finished laughing maybe you would like to see that you didn't get away scot-free either,' he derided softly.

Darcy looked up at him with puzzled eyes, following his line of vision to her breasts, the nipples standing out against the blue material like twin pebbles. 'Oh, Reed!' She fell laughingly into his arms. 'What are they going to think of us?'

'Do I really need to answer that?' he drawled, his hands threading into her hair either side of her nape as he brought his mouth down on hers.

She forgot about his family, forgot it was only

nine o'clock at night and that of course the others would know why they had come to bed so abruptly, losing herself in the magic of his kiss.

'Maybe you really are a witch,' Reed murmured against the curve of her breast as he removed the scrap of material that covered them. 'I've been imagining feasting on this milk and honey all evening!'

Darcy gasped as she felt the pleasure-pain of his mouth closing about one nipple, suckling thirstily; her legs trembled weakly and her hands grasped his shoulders to support her.

'Milk and honey!' He moaned before capturing her other breast to give it the same loving caress.

She had never experienced caresses like these before, collapsing completely as Reed's hand sought the secrets he had bared with the removal of that other scrap of material, her eyes wide with shock as she felt the touch of his mouth where his hand had just been.

Reed looked up at her concernedly. 'You don't like that? Just tell me if I go too far, if I shock you. I only want to give you pleasure!'

She felt bereft without the touch of his mouth, arching up to initiate the caress, sighing her satisfaction at the pleasure that lit up his eyes before his head bent in studied concentration.

He only relented when her whimpers of need reached screaming fulfilment, their bodies covered in a silken sheen as Reed pressed soothing kisses against her brow, her breathing laboured as she returned to sanity.

But another shock awaited her as Reed began

to move his thigh rhythmically against her; she could feel the pleasure course through her body a second time, knew that this time she wanted him inside her, his hardness taking her to that kaleidoscope of colour as he joined her there.

She bit down on her lip to stop from crying out as he gently separated that barrier that prevented the perfect joining of their bodies, feeling the tension in his shoulders where seconds ago he had been relaxed with the knowledge of the approaching satisfaction for them both.

Her eyes pleaded with him not to stop, not to question, and after a significant pause the pain went out of his eyes, the tension leaving his shoulders and back as he began to stroke deep inside her where no other man had ever been.

CHAPTER SEVEN

'IF there was one other relationship, Darcy, how did you come to me a virgin?'

She had been expecting this question since last night when she had sensed his shock at her inexperience. But even though it was now morning, the night hours, despite Reed's claim to the contrary, having seen them return to that heady delight twice more before they fell asleep in each others arms, she couldn't look him directly in the eyes as she answered him.

'He—Jason realised at the last minute that he didn't want me.' She could still remember the painful humiliation of realising she couldn't even arouse Jason enough to give him what he needed, the two of them dressing in silence afterwards, knowing that the experiment wouldn't be repeated. It hadn't been until she met Reed and realised how she felt about him that she had been grateful for her aborted affair with Jason, knew that the relationship hadn't been worthy of either of them.

Reed had left her in little doubt last night of her ability to arouse him!

'Were you in love with him?' Reed asked huskily, obviously puzzled about the whole relationship.

'I thought we—needed, each other,' she evaded. 'It just didn't work out.'

'And now?'

'I'm so glad you were the first, Reed.' She looked up at him with glowing eyes. 'It felt— right, with you.' She frowned as she saw the flicker of uncertainty in his eyes. 'Reed?' He couldn't already be regretting last night, not when it had been so beautiful!

'After the first time, when I realised that in your experience you wouldn't have taken care of such things, I took preventative measures, but that first time . . .!' He grimaced at his lack of control even after he had breached that gossamer barrier. 'I couldn't have stopped at that moment if our lives had depended on it!'

She knew what he was trying to say, and the thought of a child being made from their lovemaking was as much a shock to her as it obviously was to him. But for different reasons she was sure. She knew she didn't deserve the happiness of having Reed's baby.

'It will be all right, Reed,' she assured him as she stretched her silky length above him, thrilled as she felt him stir beneath her.

'You would tell me if it isn't?' he persisted, even as his body leapt with desire.

'Of course,' she confirmed without hesitation. 'I'm sure you would never "demand" that I marry you or threaten to take the baby away from me.' She was confident he would never be so cruel as to do the latter but she wouldn't object at all if he wanted to do the former.

'Darcy, this is serious!'

'Babies usually are,' she nodded. 'But aren't

you being a little premature?' she teased. 'We've only spent one night together.'

'Are there going to be other nights?'

Now that she had known him so completely she felt as if she would die if she didn't spend the rest of her nights with him in his arms and all of her days at his side. 'Do you want there to be?'

'What a damn silly question to ask a man in my obvious condition!' He grinned self-derisively at the movement of his desire against her thigh.

'I'm yours for as long as you want me, Reed,' she told him simply.

'Why?'

She looked at him sharply. 'Why?' she repeated slowly, not expecting this response and unnerved by it.

He nodded. 'And for God's sake don't say it's because you like and respect me!'

'But I do.' She frowned her confusion as the desire began to ebb from his body at the admission.

He drew in a ragged breath, seeming to be fighting an inner battle before he smiled at her. 'Even though I was so easy to ravage last night?'

She knew he was trying to lighten the tension that suddenly existed between them, but she also knew there was an underlying seriousness to his previous question. But it was his coy expression at the suggestion that she had ravaged him last night that was her undoing, and she returned his smile.

'Don't do that,' Reed warned urgently as she laughed. 'Or I won't be answerable for the consequences to your delectable body!'

Those 'consequences' kept them in bed another hour, and Diane and Chris were long gone by the time Darcy joined Reed in the kitchen.

She wrinkled her nose. 'Burning our breakfast?' she teased at the smell of burning.

He shook his head as he carried their breakfast out to the patio. 'There are a few forest fires going because of the length of the dry spell; the smell of the smoke from those fires carries for miles.'

'Has anyone been hurt?' she asked in concern.

'Not yet,' he shrugged. 'But it's always a danger.'

'How awful,' she frowned as she poured their coffee.

He shrugged. 'It's something you get used to when you live here.'

The smell of smoke remained all day, the numerous fires that had started all over the state making the headlines on the news that evening.

'I'll arrange for us to go home in a couple of days,' Reed told her later that night when they were comfortably stretched out in bed together, his hair damp on his brow from their heated lovemaking of minutes ago.

'Shouldn't I be the one to do that?' she teased.

His eyes darkened. 'You can't continue to be my secretary now, Darcy,' he told her quietly.

She stiffened, moving to look at him, sure he couldn't actually have said what she thought he had. 'Why on earth not?' she demanded to know in a stunned voice.

'Because we're lovers,' he stated reasoningly.

Darcy wasn't in a mood to be reasoned with! 'What possible difference does that make to my continuing as your secretary?' She was incredulous.

'I can't work with you now, Darcy,' he stated flatly.

He couldn't mean it, had to be teasing her. But she could see he wasn't by the regret in his eyes! She turned away, swinging her legs down to the floor as she sat on the side of the bed. 'You should have told me the rules of this affair before it began, Reed.' She pulled on the nightshirt she hadn't bothered to wear earlier. 'I might have thought twice about going to bed with you!'

His eyes narrowed. 'You would rather have remained my secretary?'

'I would rather be your lover *and* your secretary!' She glared across at him as she stood beside the bed.

Reed shook his head. 'It just isn't possible.'

'For heaven's sake, why not?' she demanded to know exasperatedly.

'I have a business to run,' he shrugged. 'A high-powered business that absorbs me totally during the day; I don't have the time to chase my secretary around the office!'

'Chase your——!' She broke off impatiently. 'Reed, that is so silly——'

'Is it?' he rasped. 'And just what do you know about it, Darcy?'

'I know you,' she dismissed impatiently. 'Good God, I'm hardly the type to drive *any* man insane with lust just by walking into a room!'

'That's exactly the effect you have on me,'

he bit out tightly.

'Then you must be the exception,' she said exasperatedly. 'Jason didn't even——'

'I don't want to hear about your effect on other men,' Reed cut in gratingly, getting out of bed to impatiently pull on a robe. 'All I know is that I become aroused just looking at you!'

She didn't want to stop working with him, to be reduced to just being the mistress in his life, found his whole attitude unreasonable. 'Then you've managed to hide it very well all these months!' she snapped angrily.

'No, I didn't hide it at all, you were just too naïve to notice!'

'Naïve!' she repeated furiously. 'I am not——'

'Darcy, let's not argue about this,' he sighed wearily, running a hand through the thick darkness of his hair. 'We're good together like this, so damned good, let's not do anything to spoil it.'

It was already spoilt as far as Darcy was concerned. How did he expect her to continue to make love with him now as if he hadn't just told her she would be out of a job as soon as they got back to London.

'I'm not asking you to leave straight away, Darcy,' he reasoned impatiently. 'I just want you to start looking around for another job after we get back.'

'And in the meantime?' she challenged.

He shrugged. 'We carry on as we are.'

'As we are now or as we were then?' she demanded sharply, her mouth tight.

'As we are now!' he rasped. 'I can't go back to that platonic relationship.'

'And just how long do you think you'll require me as your mistress?'

'Darcy——'

'How long, Reed?' she prompted forcefully.

His mouth thinned. 'How the hell do I know?' he snapped. 'Darcy, I'm not even sure——'

'Neither am I,' she cut in firmly. 'I'm not sure at all! You should have told me the conditions of this affair, Reed,' she bit out with controlled emotion. 'I happen to prefer being your secretary!'

'You can't mean that,' he gasped.

Of course she didn't mean that, but if she had to choose between being his mistress for a few weeks or remaining his secretary on a permanent basis, she knew she would have chosen the latter, that at least that way she could continue to be with him.

'I do mean it, Reed,' she told him flatly.

'You're upset,' he dismissed. 'A lot has happened the last few days. I should have known better than to have let this develop as quickly as it has——'

'Reed, I have been upset by the robbery and other things, but I do know what I'm saying. How can you expect me to give up my job, a job I happen to like very much, to become your mistress for a few weeks?'

'Darcy——'

She drew herself up proudly, knew she wasn't getting through to him at all. 'I think I'll make use of the other bedroom if you don't mind——'

'But I do mind.' He spun her round to face him. 'Do you have any idea how long I waited to make love to you, to——'

'For me to fall into your bed?' she finished angrily. 'You said you wanted me from the beginning, so that must make it six months, three weeks and two days!' She was so angry at his high-handedness that she didn't even care that his eyes had darkened with the anger that was usually so ominous it made her forget everything else.

'Stop putting words into my mouth, damn it,' he rasped furiously.

'I'm so sorry,' she derided hardly. 'I won't say another word. In fact, I'll be glad to make the arrangements for us to go home, it can be my last task as your secretary. And that doesn't mean I intend becoming your mistress!' she glared.

'Darcy . . .!' he groaned pleadingly.

She closed the door on him, willing herself not to be moved by his harassed confusion at her reaction. What had he expected, damn him? That she was going to let him keep her for a few weeks and then meekly go on her way to a different job and a different man when he had had enough of her!

God, it had all been so perfect last night and today, seeing a side of Reed she had never thought to see, that of the indulgent lover. But he was right, it had all happened so quickly that they hadn't had time to think about what they were doing. At least, Reed didn't seem to have done. Sometime during the day he had realised the awkwardness of working with the woman he had made his latest lover.

But as she lay miserably alone in one of the single beds, she couldn't help wondering if she had been too impulsive by turning down what he offered. This way she was out of a job, too!

But she had seen too many women go in and then just as quickly out of Reed's life the last few months to settle for the same herself. She had thought he genuinely cared for her. God, of course he cared for her, just not in the way she had hoped he would. She was here, and he had wanted her, had wanted to comfort her after the trauma she had experienced. She loved him all the more for that, could even appreciate his honesty with her now; it just wasn't enough for her.

Where did they go from here?

Reed was probably no more sure of that than she was. What a mess it all was!

'Darcy! Darcy, for God's sake wake up!'

The hand pushing at her shoulder was very insistent, and she pushed it away irritably. She was still tired, just wanted to continue sleeping.

'Darcy, you have to wake up!' That voice persisted in interrupting her dreams.

'Go away,' she mumbled, turning over to snuggle beneath the bedclothes.

'Darcy!' This time she was shaken until her eyes opened in startled accusation.

'Reed!' She glared at him, the mists of sleep taking a long time to clear. 'What time is it?' she frowned at her watch. 'My God,' she groaned when her vision cleared enough to read it. 'You should have woken me earlier, it's ten o'clock, and——'

'Darcy, we don't have the time for this.' Reed was frantically pulling open the drawers containing her clothes, pulling out several items haphazardly to throw them to her on the bed. 'Get dressed,' he ordered forcefully. 'I'll pack as many of your things as I can while I wait for you.'

She watched in stupefaction as he began to throw her belongings into her case.

'Darcy!' he rasped fiercely as he turned to see she hadn't made a move. 'For God's sake get your clothes on or I'll take you out of here as you are!'

'We're leaving now?' she queried disjointedly. 'But there aren't any flights available until later today.' She had checked before she fell asleep the previous night.

'I know that,' he rasped, snapping her case shut on the few things he had managed to throw inside. 'Let's go,' he instructed harshly. 'We don't have the time for you to dress.'

'But where are we going? Reed——'

'Darcy,' he became suddenly still, 'one of those forest fires raging out of control is heading this way. Soon. Understand?'

She was too frightened to do anything but what Reed told her after that, knowing he was as taken aback as she when they emerged from the house to the smell of trees, dry and brittle from prolonged heat, being consumed by flames, smoke settling threateningly in the air as it made their eyes sting and their throats burn.

'Chris and Diane?' she managed to gasp as Reed took one look at the flames that could be seen in the distance before running to the car.

'Chris's at work and Diane went shopping,' Reed supplied economically as he helped her into the car.

'The other people——'

'All warned.' He climbed in behind the wheel of the car.

'Reed . . .' she questioned faintly as the distant fire seemed to hold her mesmerised in its grip.

He turned to her with narrowed eyes. 'Yes?'

She wrenched her gaze away from the smoke and flames. 'Are we going to get out of this?'

His expression softened. 'You think I'm going to let anything take you from me now?' he teased lightly

'Reed, please, I'm serious!' she groaned.

'And you think I'm not?' he grated. 'After sleeping alone last night I decided that *nothing* was going to keep me from your bed in future,' he declared with a return of his usual arrogance.

Darcy looked at him searchingly, but there was no real time for questions, only action. The time for questions could come later.

CHAPTER EIGHT

WADE and Linda asked questions, Diane asked questions, but by eight o'clock that night Darcy felt too weary to want to do anything more than fall into bed.

Reed's prompt action in getting them both away to safety had been what saved them, the fire missing them by minutes as it rolled along, burning all in its way. Darcy knew she owed her life to him, that if it weren't for his calm quick-thinking the two of them would have been as black and charred as Diane and Chris's house had been when she insisted Reed drive her back, once the fire had passed on, to survey the damage. The house had been burnt to the ground, along with everything around it. One minute there had been beautiful houses and trees surrounding the tranquillity of the lake and the next there had been nothing but ashes.

Reed had cursed his stupidity in allowing her to persuade him to let her see the destruction, had insisted on taking her to hospital to be checked over for shock. After the doctor declared her fit, Reed had driven them both to Linda's house. Reed had been fully dressed when he woke her, but Darcy was still in her nightshirt hours later, and a bath and a change of clothes had never seemed so welcome.

Everything had been destroyed, and it was Chris and Diane Darcy felt most sorry for; they had lost everything to the fire. Diane accepted it, just relieved that no lives had been lost, but Chris seemed in shock when the couple arrived that evening; the two of them staying at their hotel for the moment. He spoke little during their visit, and Darcy's heart went out to him. A house was so personal, became so much a part of the people who lived in it, and the happy memories shared there had burnt along with it.

'I'm so sorry.' She moved to squeeze Chris's arm in sympathy.

He gave her a sharp look. '*You're* sorry?'

She nodded. 'This must be so painful for you.'

Emotion flickered in his eyes. 'I—Yes,' he answered abruptly. 'Diane, we should be going,' he told his wife sharply as she sat chatting with Linda and Marie.

Diane frowned at the sharpness of his voice. 'Honey, are you——'

'Let's go.' He stood up disjointedly. 'I'm sure Darcy and Reed would like to get to bed.'

'Yes, but——'

'I said let's go!' he grated forcefully, his hands clenched tensely into fists at his sides.

'I know it's been a blow for him,' Mike murmured once the other couple had left, Diane looking confused by her husband's unwarranted aggression. 'But Diane lost her home, too!'

'Leave it,' Reed advised gruffly. 'It's been a hell of a day for all of us.' He ran a hand through the dark thickness of his hair, several strands falling boyishly across his forehead. 'It will all seem a little less traumatic after a good night's sleep.'

'Well the fire has made me see sense,' Linda put in shakily. 'Life is too damned short for the type of stubbornness I've been showing lately.' She turned to her husband. 'Could I entice you to bed, my darling?' she said huskily.

Wade eyed her warily. 'You could entice me off a cliff edge, and you know it!'

'Could I entice you into giving me a baby?' she added throatily.

Her husband swallowed convulsively. 'You're sure it's what you really want? I'm not going to push you any more; the fire has also shown me how stupid I've been. I have you, what more do I want?' he dismissed.

'I'll show you, darling,' she murmured seductively. 'Let's go to bed and discuss it.' She looked pointedly at their listening audience.

'What a good idea,' Wade's arm came about her shoulders. 'Excuse us, won't you?' he mockingly addressed the rest of the family. 'My wife has something very urgent to "discuss" with me.'

'You should be so lucky,' Mike derided, giving Marie an affectionate smile as she punched him lightly on the arm. 'Come on, wife-and-a-bit, let's go home and have a cuddle!'

Darcy had been dreading and yet anticipating the time for her and Reed to go to bed, dreading it because she was no longer sure *what* Reed wanted from her, anticipating it because she knew what she could *make* him want from her, if only for a few hours. And she did need him tonight, needed to feel close to him again after the way she had clung to him after they had driven away from the fire. Sleep suddenly seemed unimportant.

She lay in the bed and watched him as he stood just inside the bathroom doorway shaving the day's growth of beard from his jaw. His movements were deft and unhurried, only the deep lines beside his eyes and mouth showing that he had found the events of the day a strain, too. He had been so much in control throughout the day that no one, including herself, seemed to have considered he might have been badly shaken, too.

'Reed.' Darcy went to him, her arms about his waist as she pressed her head against his chest. 'God, it was so awful!'

'Yes.' His arms closed about her. 'Remind me never to take you on a business trip again,' he murmured into her hair. 'So far I've managed to make you faint on the plane, be involved in a robbery, and now this damned fire,' he rasped. 'I should never have brought you here and exposed you to this!'

'You couldn't have had any idea——'

'You're going home tomorrow,' he interrupted harshly, his tone brooking no argument.

It was a warning Darcy didn't heed. 'But——'

'I've already booked the flight.'

'I see,' she frowned.

His arms contracted about her. 'This trip is something I hope you *can* forget!'

'But you haven't found out yet who's betraying

your confidences; you need me here for that,' she protested.

'Do I?' he rasped.

She frowned up at him. 'You said that you did.'

He shrugged. 'Maybe at first I thought I did. But now I just want you to get back to London and away from here.'

'You aren't coming back with me tomorrow?' She looked at him worriedly.

'I hadn't planned to.' He shook his head. 'Not unless the situation resolves itself before then.'

'Before tomorrow?' Her eyes widened. 'But——'

'Put it out of your mind, Darcy,' he instructed harshly. 'I wouldn't have brought you here at all if——' He broke off, his mouth compressing as he gave a self-impatient sigh.

'If?' she prompted softly. 'Reed——'

'Darcy, can I make love with you tonight?'

She blinked up into the harshness of his face, stunned at the emotionless way he had said that after what he had told her this morning about wanting to spend all his nights with her in future. But that had been said in the heat of the moment, danger speeding quickly towards them. And she had been frightened, oh, so frightened, and Reed's calmness then had soothed her. She could see that to him it had meant no more than that.

She could also see now that he wasn't in the mood to have his motives questioned, and after spending one miserable night without him she needed him too much to want to push him.

For her answer she stepped back from him,

slowly unfastening the buttons down the front of her shirt before pulling it over her head and dropping it on to the ground. She was unashamedly naked.

Reed drew in a ragged breath, releasing the towel that had been draped about his waist since his shower, as naked as she, his arousal strong and full. 'I don't need to tell you how much I want and need you,' he mocked drily.

'Men are at a distinct disadvantage that way,' she acknowledged throatily, running a caressing hand across his chest, her fingertips light on the brown nubs nestled there as she heard the tempo of his breathing change to a ragged sigh.

'Would you—kiss me?' he asked between clenched teeth.

She tilted her head to one side in silent query as she sensed the underlying tension beneath the request, her legs turning to jelly as she saw the pleading in his eyes, the pleasure he was already experiencing at the mercy of her questing hands.

She was sure Linda would have been shocked if she knew the use to which her carpet was put that night, Darcy and Reed sinking down to the creamy softness as they explored the valleys and curves of each others' bodies with slow delight.

It was a time for slow, lingering passion, a time to bask in the pure joy of just being alive, of being able to pleasure each other. Their bodies joined, their senses soared, that deep overwhelming pleasure holding them in its thrall until they both collapsed into the realms of Morpheus, too satiated to move.

*　　*　　*

The heat was overwhelming, the smell of smoke and burning choking in her lungs, the brightness of the flames blinding her as she instinctively threw up her arms to protect herself.

She woke bathed in perspiration, reaching out beside her in the bed for Reed, the dream so vivid she still trembled with fear. Reed wasn't lying beside her.

She moved to put on the bedside lamp, turning to the place beside her where Reed should have been. The indentation on the pillow showed that he had joined her in the bed after carrying her here, if only briefly. The bedside clock told her it was almost three o'clock in the morning; maybe he had been troubled by the same horrendous nightmare as she, and had decided to go for a walk to clear his head.

Her nightshirt had been picked up from the floor where she had thrown it earlier and was draped across the foot of the bed, and she smoothed the cotton down over her body before going in search of Reed.

The O'Neals' house was as elegant as Diane and Chris's had been, although it was in a more built-up area, with several other houses close by, although they were all in darkness now. The lounge, lit by a single lamp, was deserted; so was the kitchen, but she could hear the sound of voices coming softly from the patio that surrounded the O'Neals' swimming pool. It looked as if either Linda or Wade had joined Reed in his night-time wandering.

She came to an abrupt halt in the doorway as

she saw that Reed's companion was Chris Donavan.

Reed stood up as soon as he saw her, frowning at how pale she was. 'What happened?' He put his arm about her shoulders, solidly comforting, and so very normal in fitted denims and open-necked shirt.

'Just a bad dream,' she dismissed lightly, although she knew by the compassion that darkened his eyes that he realised it hadn't been 'just' a dream at all. 'I didn't mean to interrupt anything.' She looked curiously at Chris; the other man was as pale as she knew she was, seeming even more strained than he was earlier.

'Chris and I were only talking,' Reed assured her huskily.

She nodded. 'I just wondered where you had gone; I'll go back to bed now——'

'No!' Chris stood up forcefully, his arms tense at his side. 'Don't leave on my account,' he added in a slightly calmer voice.

Darcy moved from Reed's side to put her hand comfortingly on Chris's arm. 'I can't tell you how sorry I am that you lost your house——'

'Don't,' he choked, looking at Reed for help. 'If it hadn't been for me——'

'Darcy,' Reed cut in curtly, 'maybe you should go and put some clothes on——'

'No,' Chris told him firmly. 'Darcy has a right to hear this. She's been involved, too, by what's happened since she came here. God, she could have been killed today because of me; you both could!'

'But we weren't, Chris——'

'You can't take responsibility for an act of nature,' Darcy reasoned.

The dark eyes were shadowed with pain, his breathing ragged. 'If it hadn't been for me you and Reed wouldn't even have been here!' Chris rasped.

'Of course we— Oh!' Her eyes widened incredulously as she realised what he was saying to her. *Chris* was the one Reed was looking for? She hadn't wanted to believe that any of Reed's family was involved, but quietly intense Chris Donavan was the last one she would have suspected. 'Maybe I should leave the two of you alone to talk,' she said awkwardly, looking questioningly at Reed.

He looked at his brother-in-law. 'Chris?' he prompted softly.

'I'd like Darcy to stay and hear this,' he told them gratingly.

Reed nodded abruptly. 'We can have a drink while Darcy puts some clothes on.'

Darcy wished he would stop telling her to get dressed; the cotton nightshirt was perfectly respectable to wear in mixed company, and hearing what Chris had to say was much more important than her putting clothes on!

'Darcy!' he prompted harshly as she made no move to leave the room.

She followed the direction of his gaze as it rested pointedly on the length of her thigh revealed by the split up the seam on each side of the garment to allow her freedom of movement.

As if Chris was in any sort of mood to notice, let alone be attracted to her!

But Reed looked ready to argue the point, and so with a sigh she gave in, promising them she would be back in a few minutes.

Chris. She couldn't believe it. She couldn't understand *why* he had done it. He seemed to have everything he could possibly want already: a beautiful and loving wife, a thriving hotel; what could have prompted him to use Reed the way he had?

The two men had moved into the lounge when she returned from putting on denims and a loose cotton blouse. Silently accepting the glass of whisky Reed handed her, she sat down with it in her hand; maybe she would have need of it later!

Now that she had put in her contact lenses she could clearly see just how ill Chris looked, his cheeks pale and hollow, his eyes seeming to have sunk into dark sockets. He tightly gripped his glass of whisky in both hands as he stared off into space.

'Chris,' Reed prompted huskily.

The other man seemed to notice Darcy's return for the first time, taking a swallow of the burning alcohol. It was evidence as to how disturbed he was that he didn't even wince as it went down his throat.

'I have to commend you on your control, Reed,' he rasped. 'If the positions had been reversed I would have swung my fists first and asked questions later!'

'The fists could still swing,' Reed grated. 'Not for myself, but for Darcy. And Diane.'

Chris seemed to become even greyer and more haggard at the mention of his wife. 'I never meant for anyone to get hurt. I just——'

'Start at the beginning, Chris,' Reed said curtly.

'The beginning?' Chris gave a harsh laugh. 'I'd have to go back years!'

'Then do it!' Reed snapped, obviously at the end of his patience.

The other man drew in a ragged breath. 'College,' he bit out. 'I had to work my way through; your father helped you with your expenses——'

'Hell, you can't have held that against me all these years!' Reed said disbelievingly.

'I didn't hold it against you at all,' Chris dismissed tautly. 'I'm just trying to point out the differences in our backgrounds. I've always had to fight and claw for what I wanted out of life; things always came easier to you. Not that you ever took your good fortune for granted; you always appreciated how lucky you had been. And for some reason you made me your friend——'

'I like you,' Reed put in gruffly. 'I always have.'

'You were the bright star even then, and I bathed in your reflected glory. I even had a few successes of my own,' he remembered harshly. 'You drew me into the warmth of your family, encouraged my partnership with Mike, approved wholeheartedly of my marriage to Diane.'

'I told you,' Reed's eyes were narrowed, 'I liked you.'

Chris nodded, sighing heavily. 'The partnership with Mike was a success, the marriage to Diane even more so—I love her so damned much,' he told them shakily.

'You've acted like it the last few months!' Reed bit out scornfully.

'Reed,' Darcy gently rebuked. She could see exactly the picture Chris was painting, had felt a little that way herself the last few days, as if to be admitted into the Hunter family was to enter a charmed circle. It could be daunting.

Chris gave another ragged sigh. 'I wanted to be more than just Mike's partner, your friend, and Diane's husband; I needed something of my own. The hotel seemed the perfect solution.'

'It's one of the most exclusive in the area.' Reed looked at him with puzzled eyes.

'Yes,' Chris told them heavily. 'But exclusivity costs money. I know that sounds ridiculous, but it happens to be true. I hit difficulty just before Christmas, and borrowed money I couldn't pay back any other way than by handing over the hotel itself.'

'You could have asked me for the money, damn it!' Reed flared.

'No,' Chris bit out. 'I couldn't do that.'

'Why the hell not?'

'Because the hotel was *mine*,' Chris pleaded, willing him to understand the streak of pride that wouldn't let him ask for money on a venture that belonged solely to him.

'So instead you took pay-offs for information received—from me?' Reed said disgustedly.

'It was better than asking you for money,' Chris defended.

'I don't see it that way,' Reed scorned. 'I doubt anyone else will either!'

'Reed, you don't have to tell anyone else,' Darcy reasoned.

'No, I don't,' he acknowledged softly, looking at his brother-in-law.

'But I do,' Chris put in harshly. 'I got myself into this mess and now I've got to get myself out of it. I only realised a couple of days ago that you were on to something,' he admitted heavily. 'When Maud telephoned she seemed surprised at how—close, the two of you were here when you had acted like just employer and employee in London.' He grimaced. 'I should have realised earlier what you were doing, I suppose, but it didn't even occur to me.'

'Too busy with your success?' Reed scorned.

'I didn't enjoy doing what I did, Reed.' Chris looked at him for understanding. 'I was approached, I needed the money, and——'

'You could have said no!'

'I could have,' the other man acknowledged heavily. 'And then I would have lost the hotel, the house, maybe even Diane. I love her so damn much,' he repeated shakily. 'And now I've lost her anyway.'

'Not necessarily,' Reed said softly.

Dark eyes looked at him sharply, and Darcy looked at Reed, too. He was no longer angry; only regret was reflected in dark green eyes. She felt for him that his worst nightmare had come true, that he had been betrayed by one of his best friends. But she had also witnessed the fondness Chris had shown for him the last few days, knew the other man had to have been desperate to have risked so much.

'What do you mean?' Chris questioned abruptly.

Reed sighed. 'I'm the only one that's really been affected in this, and I have no intention of letting my knowledge go any further than here and now. I'm sure Darcy feels the same way.' He gave her a slight smile as he correctly guessed her thoughts. 'What you did wasn't illegal——'

'It was disgusting,' Chris corrected harshly. 'I divulged information you were sure would go no further——'

'They were only lost business deals,' Reed dismissed. 'The family is at risk now.'

'How long have you known it was me?' Chris asked in a fatalistic voice.

Darcy had been wondering the same thing. Now that Chris had actually confessed, Reed didn't seem surprised, just disappointed—that his suspicions had finally been confirmed?

Reed gave a grimace of regret. 'Almost since we got here,' he admitted, the expression in his eyes asking for Darcy's forgiveness at the deception. 'As Darcy so rightly pointed out, Wade was just angry at Linda because she refused to have children, and that was no reason to do this. And Diane told Darcy the hotel was having some financial difficulty; when I asked you how business was you told me it was great, that you were thinking of expanding. I know Diane doesn't lie,' he added simply.

'No,' Chris acknowledged heavily. 'She's never seen any reason to be less than totally honest.'

'Why the hell didn't you come to me?' Reed demanded again impatiently. 'It's what families are for, damn it, to pull together in a crisis!'

'You had made your life in England——'

'I was only a phone call away!'

'It was my problem, not yours.'

Reed gave a ragged sigh. 'You're my best friend, my sister's husband; I thought we were close enough for you to have come to me about this.'

Maybe they had been once, Darcy realised, but Reed's years in England had taken their toll on what had once been a very close friendship. Darcy could feel those almost invisible chains of family closeness tightening about him, pulling him away from England and back to America. She knew by Reed's grim expression that he could feel them, too.

'I wish that I had now,' Chris sighed. 'What do we do now?'

'I deliberately waited until Mom was away on her cruise before coming over here,' Reed told him harshly. 'You know what this would do to her if she were to find out?'

Chris's throat moved convulsively. 'I never meant to hurt anyone,' he groaned. 'Least of all Maud; she's always been like a mother to me.'

'And with her weak heart a shock like this could kill her,' Reed rasped. 'Only the three of us actually know about this——'

'Four.' A voice came from the hallway, as Diane stepped forward into the light. 'I heard it all,' she told her husband simply at his pained gasp as he came slowly to his feet.

'Diane . . .!' Chris's dismay at her presence here came out as a strangulated protest.

All the laughter had gone from the deep green eyes as Diane continued to look at her husband, his pain mirrored by the disillusionment in those dull green eyes. 'I woke up when you got out of bed,' she explained flatly. 'You seemed so upset earlier, I was worried when you got dressed and left without telling me you were going. So I—I followed you.' She gave a pained wince. 'I'm glad now that I did.'

'Diane——'

'I would have told you anyway, Diane,' Chris firmly cut in on Reed's reasoning voice. 'I couldn't have kept something like this from you.'

Darcy felt uncomfortably as if she were intruding on something that was completely private between husband and wife; she looked uncertainly at Reed. Surely what followed, in the light of Reed's decision to forgive and forget, was completely private to Diane and Chris?

'Darcy and I are going back to bed.' Reed's arm came about her shoulders as he faced the other couple. 'I just want you to know that as far as we're concerned this goes no further than the four of us.'

'Thank you.' Diane squeezed his arm, her eyes brimming with tears.

Steady green eyes forced the other man to meet his gaze. 'There's an unconditional loan waiting for you whenever you want it,' he told Chris huskily. 'And don't say you don't want it,' he warned harshly. 'I'd give you the damned money but I know you wouldn't take it; the loan can be drawn up legally.'

Darcy said nothing on the way back to their bedroom, although she watched Reed anxiously as they undressed and climbed back into bed. She silently held him cradled against her breast, hoping to be the comforter to the pain she knew he was feeling.

'I'd hoped——' He broke off. 'I tried not to believe——' He stopped a second time as his voice broke emotionally.

'He never really meant to hurt you, Reed,' she reasoned huskily.

'I know that,' he rasped, holding her tightly.

'Do you—— Do you think Diane will stay with him?'

'Yes,' he answered without hesitation. 'She loves him.'

'And you're going to help him.'

He drew in a ragged breath. 'One thing this has shown me is that whether I want it or not I have responsibilities to the family. They aren't weak, they're just human. As a family unit we're invincible; apart . . .' He sighed heavily. 'I have to move back here.'

She knew that, had known from the time they arrived here that Reed needed his family as much as they needed him; this episode with Chris just confirmed it.

But where did that leave her?

CHAPTER NINE

SHE had always known her parents were good people, but that weekend as she basked in their undemanding love she realised just how nice they were. She hadn't visited them much in the last seven months; she had found that the familiarity of everything at home reminded her too much of all that she had tried to leave behind when she moved to London, away from anything that could remind her of Jayne—and Jason.

But on her return alone from America she had known she needed to get away, and her parents' warmth beckoned her as never before. How different was the quiet tranquillity of her own family compared to the boisterous Hunters; one not preferable to the other, they were just different.

She felt different herself from her last visit home; being in America with Reed this time had changed her. She didn't know in quite what way, but she no longer felt the need to run from anything unpleasant. She was even learning to cope with more than one thing at a time, more than one trauma at a time!

Then, as confused and unsettled as she was about any future relationship with Reed, she met Jason while out shopping with her mother!

She could see the panicked distress in her

mother's face as she seemed about to make their excuses, but had smoothly taken over the situation as she invited Jason to join them both for coffee. For a moment he had hesitated, and then he had nodded reluctant acceptance.

It was the first time Darcy had seen him for almost a year, and after a stilted beginning they had talked openly, much to her mother's consternation, as she made her excuses on the pretext of going to the shop next door. Darcy had felt as if at least one of her ghosts from the past had been laid to rest by the time she rejoined her mother twenty minutes later.

She returned to London ready to accept whatever Reed had decided.

He had stayed on with his family over the weekend, Darcy insisting it would be better for all concerned if she went ahead and returned to London as planned, feeling too much like an intruder into what was, after all, a private family matter.

She had no doubt that Reed would tell her what decisions and plans he had made for the future when he was good and ready.

He wasn't in his office when she arrived on Monday morning, and as she wasn't even sure he was in the country yet, having received no word from him, she began the morning routine of dealing with the mail, assuming that he would be in some time today.

'How did you manage to get that tan when you should have been working?'

She smiled at Marc as he sauntered into the

room wearing the customary faded denims and open-necked shirt. 'It wasn't all work,' she murmured softly, remembering only too well how little work had been involved in her time spent in Orlando.

'No?' Marc made himself comfortable on the side of her desk, his blue eyes probing into hers. 'Reed hasn't done the unforgivable and stolen my girl, has he?' There was an underlying seriousness to the teasing question.

'Stolen' wasn't quite the way she would have put it, not when she had always belonged to Reed. But it was near enough to the truth to make her blush as she turned away. 'How many models did you date while I was away?' she derided.

'One or two,' he drawled in confirmation. 'And don't change the subject.'

She continued to channel her attention on the build up of mail that had been waiting for her. 'I didn't realise I had.'

Lean fingers rested against her chin as he tilted her face up to his. 'You realised,' Marc said slowly. 'Darcy, what happened in——'

'When the two of you have quite finished gazing into each other's eyes, perhaps we can get some work done around here!' rasped the all-too-familiar voice of Darcy's boss. She couldn't think of him as her lover when he spoke in that tone!

Darcy turned to him with stricken eyes, knowing how damning the scene he had walked in on must look to him. He looked furious, the lines of strain more pronounced, as if finding

Marc supposedly drooling all over her were the last straw after the tense few days he had just had.

Marc looked unperturbed, as usual. 'Would you believe I was just checking Darcy had both contact lenses in?' he drawled mockingly.

'No, I wouldn't!'

Darcy winced as the outer door closed behind Reed with a slam that made it rattle on its hinges. 'Reed, I——'

'Don't you have any work to do?' He glared at the other man, completely ignoring Darcy.

'Plenty,' Marc answered cheerfully, making no move to get up off the desk.

'Then I would appreciate it if you could stop seducing my secretary long enough to go and do it!' Reed rasped coldly. 'Haven't the two of you had enough of each other over the weekend?'

'Reed . . .?'

'Well?' Again he ignored her, glaring at the younger man.

'Can a man ever have enough of a woman like Darcy?' Marc taunted.

Darcy felt as if all the breath had been forced from her body at this blatant challenge after what he had already guessed had occurred in America between Reed and herself. Marc's warped sense of humour was the last thing she needed today. 'I spent the weekend——'

'Really, Darcy,' Marc reproved huskily. 'A lady doesn't "kiss and tell", either!'

'Marc, would you just shut up,' she told him exasperatedly. 'This isn't funny.'

He grinned. 'It is from where I'm sitting.'

'Re-*eed*!' she gasped shrilly as Marc found he was no longer 'sitting' at all, but held at the end of Reed's clenched fist in his shirt-front, their faces, Reed's furiously angry, Marc's mildly surprised by the attack, only inches apart. 'Reed, put him down,' she begged desperately.

'I'll *knock* him down if he doesn't get the hell out of here,' he bit out through tight lips before slowly releasing the other man.

'Okay, I'll go.' Marc held up his hands defensively, laughter still lurking in the depths of his eyes. 'You could have warned me just how little "work" it was, Darcy,' he derided.

'Marc, I'm sorry——'

'Hey,' he grinned, enjoying himself immensely. 'Don't worry about it. I can assure you I'm not about to go and throw myself out of my studio window or anything drastic like that.'

'You're only two floors up,' she reminded him drily.

'You see, what good would it do?' he laughed softly. 'If all I did was break a leg I'd be denying all those other beautiful women the benefit of my—company, for months.'

Reed moved to hold the door open. 'Get out of here,' he ordered flatly.

Marc turned to wink at Darcy as he reached the door. 'Give me a call next time you're available,' he invited huskily.

She was well aware that the provocative statement only meant he wanted her to let him know Reed hadn't actually resorted to violence on her once Marc had left her alone with the other man; she was also aware that that wasn't how it must have sounded to Reed. Marc was a devil!

Reed closed the door behind the other man with suppressed violence. 'What the hell do you mean by going from me straight to him?' he challenged viciously.

'I spent the weekend——'

'I don't want to hear the details, damn you,' he snapped, breathing hard in his agitation.

'Reed, you aren't thinking straight——'

'I'm trying not to *think* at all,' he ground out. 'But it isn't easy!'

Darcy was angry, she would guess just as angry as Reed was, but she also knew that if she lost her temper with him the situation would never be resolved. 'Reed, no matter what assumption you've come to about Marc and I, or what he let you believe, I did not spend the weekend with him,' she stated calmly.

Uncertainty flickered in the stormy green depths of his eyes, and she knew she had been wise not to fire his temper any more than it already was. 'I called you,' he bit out. 'Several times during the last couple of days. You were never there.'

She sighed. 'I went home to visit my parents for the weekend.'

His eyes narrowed disbelievingly. 'You never go home,' he accused.

'That isn't true, Reed,' she rebuked with a frown. 'Admittedly I haven't been home all that often——'

'Once in the seven months you've worked for me!'
She frowned. 'I haven't been counting——'

'Well I have!'

'Why?' She eyed him suspiciously.

'Did you see Jason while you were at home?'
He didn't answer her question.

The colour in her cheeks gave him his answer.
'We did meet——'

'I'll be in my office if you need me,' he cut in
coldly. 'Otherwise I don't want to be disturbed.'

Her first instinct was to follow him, but she
didn't know what she would say even if she did
do that. She had explained about Marc, but there
was no way she could have explained about
Jason.

Marc came into her office once he knew Reed
was safely out to lunch. 'If Mohammed won't
come to the mountain.'

Darcy glared at him. 'You have all the
sensitivity of a mountain!'

'Hey, don't blame me for Reed's insecurities,'
he chided lightly, sitting in the chair opposite her
desk to stretch out his long legs in front of him.

'That's ridiculous. Reed is the most self-
confident man I know,' she scorned.

'Except when it comes to you,' Marc drawled.

'What on earth do you mean?' she frowned.

He shrugged. 'If you have a day to spare I
could probably skim the surface, but——'

'Marc, what are you talking about?' she sighed
wearily, the volcanic morning she had spent with
Reed meaning she didn't have her usual patience
to cope with Marc's innuendoes now.

'The way Reed feels about you.'

'I don't know what you mean,' she dismissed impatiently.

'No.' He smiled acknowledgment of the fact, shaking his head. 'The two of you have become lovers and you still know nothing about his feelings!'

Wings of colour highlighted her cheeks at the statement. 'We——'

'Yes?' Marc quirked mocking brows as he sensed she had been about to deny his claim. 'God, the man waits months to make love to you and then he makes a complete hash of it!' he burst out disgustedly. 'Now if it had been me—— But then, you aren't in love with me,' he sighed dismissively.

The colour deepened in her cheeks. 'I——'

'Uh uh,' he warned lightly. 'It's naughty to tell lies.'

She pulled a face at him. 'When did you get to be so wise and all-knowing?'

'And being nasty to me isn't going to help either,' he told her good-naturedly. 'Even an insensitive idiot like me can see you're in love with Reed.'

'Then why did you invite me out if you knew I felt that way about him?' She frowned her puzzlement.

Marc grinned again. 'I could say I decided to lend a hand to true love and romance and pushed Reed into action because of jealousy and desperation,' he drawled. 'But then *I'd* be lying,' he admitted lightly. 'I'm not above trying to take advantage of another man's stupidity.'

It was impossible to remain angry with this man, he just never took anyone or anything seriously! 'You're impossible!' she told him, half-laughing, half-serious. 'If I had any sense I'd ask you to leave.'

'Ah, but then you would never get to hear how Reed feels about you; he certainly doesn't seem to be about to tell you!' Marc scorned impatiently.

Darcy sighed. 'I know how Reed feels about me; I remind him of his mother.'

'His *what*?' Marc burst into peals of stunned laughter.

'It isn't funny.' She glared at him.

'Reed finally took you to bed and then told you you remind him of his *mother*?'

'No,' she rebuked crossly. 'I just know he finds my forgetfulness as irritating as he finds his mother's vagueness.'

Marc shook his head disgustedly. 'I don't know what went on in Florida—not all of it, anyway,' he added mockingly. 'But I thought Reed had more sophistication than to have allowed things to have deteriorated between you this badly. He——'

'Are you back again?' Reed scowled at them both from the doorway. 'If you want to flirt with my secretary, Marc, do it in your own time, not mine!' His gaze raked contemptuously over Darcy's pale face before he stormed into the inner office.

Marc whistled through his teeth. 'Remind me to put on my asbestos suit the next time I come up here.'

Darcy bit back her own dismay at how damning Marc being up here again during Reed's absence must look to him. 'He has things on his mind,' she excused absently. 'Family pressures.'

'Are congratulations in order?' Marc's gaze slid pointedly to the flatness of her stomach.

'Marc, we only made love for the first time last week; don't you think that's a little too soon to know about something like that?' She closed her eyes with a groan as she saw the satisfaction gleaming in his mischievous blue eyes. 'All right, I walked right into that one,' she acknowledged huskily. 'But I can assure you that that is not what Reed has on his mind at the moment,' she told him firmly.

'Rubbish. "That" is always on a man's mind. Any man with red blood flowing through his veins, that is. And Reed has more than his fair share!'

'Women, or red blood flowing through his veins?' she derided.

'Both!'

'I know all about his women, Marc,' she sighed. 'But I can assure you he isn't even thinking about one of them at the moment.' In fact she had been rather hurt by the fact that Reed hadn't even attempted to confide in her about what had happened in Orlando after she had left. She had been so closely involved, it wouldn't have hurt him to at least tell her if Diane and Chris's marriage was going to survive the trauma.

As for the decision he had made four days ago

about moving back to Florida, he hadn't mentioned that again either. All he seemed to want to do was jump to conclusions about Marc and her.

'Stop frowning, you'll get wrinkles,' Marc told her lightly. 'Would you care to discuss Reed's family crisis?' he invited interestedly.

'No.' She smiled to take the sting out of her refusal to confide in him.

'I thought you might say that,' he grimaced, standing up. 'Ah well, back to work, I suppose.' He stretched lazily.

'You were going to tell me how Reed feels about me,' she prompted softly.

Deep blue eyes brimmed with laughter. 'Oh, I couldn't do that, Darcy,' he refused mockingly. 'It's against the gentleman's code of ethics to the rest of his sex.'

'*You* aren't a gentleman!' she pointed out scathingly.

'True,' he mused. 'But if Reed is too stupid to do his own talking, I don't think I should do it for him. I do have a word of advice, though.' He bent to whisper conspiratorially.

Darcy looked at him hopefully. 'Yes?'

'Seduction.'

She frowned. 'What about it?'

Marc gave an impatient sigh. 'I'm beginning to think the two of you deserve each other!' he said disgustedly. 'Get in there and take your clothes off,' he said, gesturing towards Reed's office. 'If he doesn't take you right then and there on the couch, give up and come downstairs to me!'

She couldn't help laughing once again at his

absurdity. 'And you'll make love to me?'

'Yes,' he grinned. 'You certainly catch on fast when you want to, Darcy.'

She shook her head regretfully in answer to his 'advice'. 'If Reed wants me he's going to have to make the first move.'

'Pride goes before a fall,' Marc derided.

Darcy shrugged. 'Sometimes pride is all that you have left.'

'Keep your chin up, Darcy.' Marc bent and kissed her lightly on the mouth.

She glanced nervously towards the inner door; the way her luck was running today Reed should have walked out right in the middle of that kiss. He didn't. She looked up to catch Marc's knowing smile, her own lips curving rather sheepishly.

Her smile faded as soon as Marc closed the door behind him on his way out.

Pride. If it were only that that stood between herself and Reed then she knew she wouldn't hesitate to do as Marc suggested and go into Reed's office now and throw herself on his mercy. But there were too many uncertainties between them.

Not that that was apparent as the afternoon progressed, with Reed conducting business as usual. He was in with a colleague when the outer door opened to admit Samantha Duval. Darcy stiffened as the woman Reed had been seeing before they left for Florida came to stand in front of her desk, her grace and elegance dominating the room.

Like all of Reed's women, Samantha was flawlessly beautiful, with a glorious cascade of red hair, lively blue eyes, pouting red lips, a creamy complexion, and the sort of body most models would kill for. As a fashion consultant, her clothes were always impeccably elegant.

Darcy felt like the sweet little-girl-next-door compared to this woman.

'Darcy,' the other woman greeted her in a friendly voice.

God, the woman even *sounded* sexy! 'Reed's busy at the moment, but——'

'Oh, I don't want to disturb him,' Samantha dismissed in a light voice. 'I just came to deliver this.' She put a box very similar in shape to a shoe-box on top of Darcy's desk.

The woman brought him presents! Maybe she had baked him a cake? Somehow this woman looked too damned sexy to be able to cook, too! Was that being prejudiced—or just plain bitchy? She decided it was a little of both.

'Are you sure you wouldn't like to see him?' she offered, feeling guilty about her thoughts. After all, what had the woman ever done to her, except be Reed's choice of woman. 'I could buzz through and——'

'No need.' Samantha shook her head, frowning as she gazed at Darcy's necklace. 'Did Reed give you that?' she asked interestedly.

Another one! 'It was a birthday present,' she supplied reluctantly. Why was everyone so interested in the unicorn necklace?

'It's lovely.' The other woman nodded. 'You

should see Reed's collection——' She broke off, a purely speculative gleam in her eyes. 'But then I suppose you have,' she realised, nodding slowly.

'Sorry?' Darcy frowned her puzzlement.

'It doesn't matter,' Samantha dismissed warmly. 'Just tell Reed he forgot this when he was at my flat earlier.' She touched the box before lifting her hand in parting, her perfume so elusively feminine it was barely perceptible once she had left the room.

Earlier? Reed had been at the woman's flat earlier. Lunchtime? He had gone out for a couple of hours of bed and whatever else Samantha Duval had offered and he had the nerve to return to the office and lash out angrily at Marc and herself for *flirting*!

My God, she had had enough of this! If Reed thought he could calmly go back to his former lover and forget what had happened between the two of them in Florida, he was going to realise she couldn't accept that as she was obviously supposed to. She wasn't just a convenient body, damn it, and it was time he realised that their lovemaking was one thing she would *never* forget!

The light of battle flowed bright and strong in her eyes as she marched into the adjoining room without knocking first, ignoring the surprise on the face of the man seated opposite Reed as she slapped the box Samantha had left on the desk in front of Reed.

'Yours,' she bit out angrily. 'With the compliments of Miss Samantha Duval. Who you apparently visited at her flat at lunchtime——'

'Darcy——'

'I haven't finished!' she rasped furiously, pushing him back down in his chair as he went to stand up. 'I'll admit I'm new to the rules of these boss/secretary affairs, but I—I'm sorry.' Her eyes shot flames at Roy Benedict as he gasped his surprise. 'Have I shocked you?' she scorned.

'Er—No,' he assured her uncomfortably, sinking down in his chair in the obvious hope of being ignored during the rest of what promised to be a fiery encounter.

'Darcy——'

'As I was saying . . .' Once again she cut across Reed's protest. 'I'm new to these relationships, but even I didn't expect you to go back to Samantha today. All day I've been putting your moodiness with me down to the problem you have in Florida, when really it was just your way of telling me it was over between us! Well let me tell you I'm sick of being treated like an idiot, I'm sick of obscure comments being made about this damned necklace you gave me——'

'Samantha?' he prompted huskily.

'Yes!' Her eyes flashed as she reached up to unclasp the necklace. 'And most of all I'm sick of you, Reed Hunter!' She slapped the necklace down next to the box on his desk. 'I love you— Oh, yes, I do,' she insisted as he went to speak. 'And I want you. But I don't have to accept your affairs with other women or the high-handed way you've been treating me today! Now if I've been wrong and you do still want me then you're going to have to come and get me!'

'Darcy!'

'I mean it, Reed.' She turned at the door, breathing hard in her distress as she faced him where he now stood across the room. 'You're bad-tempered and arrogant, but I still want you. If you want me, too, you'll stop seeing Samantha and then you'll find me and ask me to marry you. I might even accept!'

CHAPTER TEN

DID they make bigger fools than her! She didn't think so; no one else *could* be this stupid.

She had *never* acted that way before over anything, never demanded anything from anyone in that arrogant way. Reed was going to think her even more of an idiot than he had before.

Reed. He had looked so stunned by her outburst, as if he couldn't believe what he was seeing and hearing. Probably because he hadn't! He was going to be furious at her for the way she had embarrassed him in front of his business colleague. But he had to find her first, she thought thankfully.

'Here.' Marc held out a strong cup of coffee in front of her, grimacing as she sipped the syrupy brew without seeming to notice the three teaspoonsful of sugar he had put in it. 'I take it you haven't come down here so that I can make love to you?' he teased.

She shook her head. 'I'm hiding out.'

'From Reed?' He raised dark blond brows.

'Yes.' She trembled slightly.

'Somehow he never struck me as the sort to turn into a sex-fiend at the sight of a woman's naked body.'

She shook her head. 'I didn't take your "advice",' she derided impatiently. 'Instead I lost my temper with him and——'

'*You* did?' Marc looked incredulous.

Her mouth firmed. 'He spent his lunchbreak with Samantha Duval.'

'Sure?'

'The woman told me so herself!'

'And Sammy isn't the bitchy sort,' Marc murmured thoughtfully, holding up his hands defensively as Darcy glared at him. 'Can I help it if I knew her before Reed did?'

'You could try telling me what a bitch she is— even if it isn't true!' In fact, she had quite liked the woman—the only thing she hadn't liked had been her involvement with Reed!

'All right, she's a bitch.' Marc shrugged. 'A thieving seductress who——'

'She isn't,' Darcy sighed. 'But she is too good for Reed,' she added angrily.

'Now there I have to agree with you——'

'What do you mean?' she snapped indignantly.

'Any woman is too good for him,' Marc dismissed. 'The man is obviously a fool, and——'

'He is not!' she defended. 'He— What am I doing?' she groaned, looking totally bewildered.

Marc grinned. 'Acting like a woman in love! "Hell hath no fury like a woman"; I won't say "scorned" because I don't believe Reed has done that,' he added slowly. 'But God help anyone else who tries to malign the slow-witted lover; they're likely to get their eyes scratched out. Women are strange creatures——'

'You mean men are as fickle as alley-cats!' Her eyes flashed. 'Any woman will do!'

Marc blew softly through his teeth. 'I never

would have thought Reed was this stupid.' He shook his head. 'What exactly did Samantha say to you?'

'You mean before or after she put the cake-box on my desk?' Darcy scorned.

'Cake?' Marc looked totally blank at this disclosure. 'What cake?'

'The one she cooked for Reed. At least, I presume it was a cake . . .' She trailed off as Marc shook his head in firm denial. 'She can't cook,' she stated flatly.

'Nothing edible.' He pursed his lips thoughtfully. 'I wonder what was in the box?'

'A bomb, I hope!' Darcy snapped resentfully.

Marc grinned. 'I know it's trite to say you're beautiful when you're angry, but you are, Darcy. All your freckles stand out on your nose, and——'

'I have already had my unflattering resemblance to the youngest member of the Walton family remarked upon, thank you!' she bit out tautly.

'Reed again?' he quirked his eyebrows.

'Yes!'

'The man should get a zero for diplomacy!' Marc grimaced. 'Personally, I find these freckles as sexy as hell—so does Reed.' He pounced knowingly as the fiery colour highlighted her cheeks.

'You're supposed to be on my side, Marc,' she accused heatedly.

'I don't take sides, especially between a woman I happen to care about very much and my financial business partner!'

'Mercenary!'

'Yep!' He grinned good-naturedly. 'Reed's made a mess of this, Darcy,' he acknowledged lightly. 'But maybe you should have given him a chance to explain.'

'Explain?' She stood up forcefully. 'How can he explain away making love to another woman during his lunchbreak!'

'Well I know how I'd explain it, but—saved by the bell!' He grimaced at her increasingly furious expression before lifting the receiver of the ringing telephone. 'Yes. How are you?' he smoothly greeted his caller while Darcy moved a polite distance away to stare out of the window as she gave him privacy.

She had ruined things irrevocably between Reed and herself. Perhaps there had been a reasonable explanation for his visit to Samantha Duval at lunchtime—although she couldn't think of one!

'We probably *aren't* high enough for you to do any lasting damage,' Marc murmured behind her as she contemplated the street below without really seeing it.

She turned to give him a wan smile. 'I found out long ago that I don't have suicidal tendencies.' She had realised two years ago that she didn't have the will to die, that despite what she might have wished at the time her mind and body refused to accept the idea. 'I really should be going now——'

'What are you going to do?' Marc probed gently.

'Short-term, go home. Long-term, look for another job.' She shrugged ruefully.

'I know of a job that might be going if you're interested.'

'You already have a receptionist,' she smiled.

'Oh, it isn't with me.' He shook his head. 'I have this friend who makes blue movies—you should see your face!' he taunted with a chuckle. 'The laugh Reed and I had about your assumption that first day you came down here!' He grinned.

'One of the few times Reed has found my stupidity amusing,' she said dully.

'Darcy——' He turned to the door as it opened, a narrow-eyed Reed standing in the doorway. 'It's about time you got down here,' he rebuked. 'I was having difficulty stopping her from leaving.'

Darcy had become frozen to the spot at the first sight of Reed, but she turned accusing eyes on Marc at his admission. 'You told him I was here?' she gasped in disbelief.

He shrugged. 'He asked.'

'When?'

'Just now, on the telephone.'

It hadn't even occurred to her that the call could be from Reed, although she had to admit she had been too lost in her own thoughts to take much notice of Marc's end of the conversation.

'Traitor!' she accused, glancing nervously across at Reed. What was he going to do now?

'Did you make love to Sammy at lunchtime?' Marc asked the other man curiously, unmoved by Darcy's burning anger.

'Is that what you thought?' Reed frowned at Darcy.

'Don't try and deny it——'

'Darcy, could we go somewhere a little more private and discuss this?' He looked pointedly at the curiously listening Marc.

'I'll try my best not to be offended by your rude assumption that I'm in the least interested in your conversation,' Marc told them haughtily as he unhooked his jacket from the hanger behind the door. 'And as I doubt you could persuade Darcy to go anywhere with you right now, Reed, I'll leave my studio to the two of you.' He shrugged into the leather jacket. 'A word of advice . . .' He paused at the open door. 'The couch over by the wall is the most comfortable. And I expect the first boy to be named after me!' He could be heard whistling as he walked down the corridor to the lift.

'Name the first——? Oh!' Darcy gave a pained grimace, avoiding Reed's gaze. 'His sense of humour could definitely do with improving!' She turned back to her perusal of the street below, scowling at Marc as he looked up and waved to her before climbing into a taxi. So much for friendship; he had left her to the wolf!

'I don't find anything funny about the idea of your having my child.' Reed spoke from close behind her, too close.

'No,' she acknowledged heavily. 'It certainly wouldn't be funny.'

'Darcy, won't you turn and look at me?' he encouraged throatily.

If she turned she would step straight into his arms, and she couldn't do that. 'I'm sorry for what I did earlier; I didn't mean to embarrass you in front of Mr Benedict.'

'Didn't you?' he mused.

'No!'

'I wasn't in the least embarrassed, Darcy——'

'I suppose the two of you had a laugh about the way a mere secretary became so emotional over what was, after all, just a physical diversion,' she went on, voicing her pain and disillusionment.

'Darcy.' His hands on her arms turned her to face him. 'You know that isn't what happened between us in Orlando. It meant much more than that.'

'Did it?' She still avoided his gaze. 'You've told me nothing about Chris and Diane, went to another woman as soon as you got back——'

'I've been too damned mad at you since you told me you saw Jason over the weekend to think of anything else, especially after I'd walked in on you and Marc together this morning!'

'I only said I'd seen Jason, not that I went to bed with him,' she defended.

'I didn't go to bed with Sammy at lunchtime either,' he told her gently.

She looked up at him with searching eyes. 'You went to her flat . . .'

'To tell her in person that I wouldn't be seeing her again,' he said softly. 'I owed her that much at least. The box contained a few of my things that had accumulated at her place the last month or so.'

Darcy frowned. 'She didn't seem—upset.'

His mouth quirked. 'At the thought of not seeing me again?' He shook his head. 'But then she doesn't love me, Darcy,' he added softly, hesitantly.

Bright wings of colour flooded her cheeks. Had she really told him she loved him in the heat of her anger? Yes, she had. And he *had* come and found her!

'And I mean to marry you, too, if you'll have me,' he said huskily as her stricken gaze clashed with his. 'I love you very much, Darcy Faversham.'

'You do?'

His expression became so gently loving at her uncertainty that Darcy felt like crying. 'We still have so many things to talk out between us, but I think all of them can wait until you've answered my proposal.'

'I don't think you actually made one, but when you do the answer is yes!' She threw her arms about him as she raised her face for his kiss. 'Oh, yes . . .'

It was so much more than she had ever hoped for, sure that after her outburst earlier she had lost her chance of any sort of relationship with Reed. She hadn't dreamt he loved her in return.

Marc was right, the couch by the wall was the more comfortable of the two, but neither Darcy nor Reed felt the inclination to take full advantage of its comfort, content with the deeply satisfying kisses that left them shaking for more; their talk had to come first.

'Let's go back to my apartment,' Reed murmured against her temple as he nuzzled against her. 'I have a present waiting for you there.'

'My mother warned me about men like you!'

'It's an engagement present,' he chided lovingly. 'Somewhere during the muddle the last few days have been I had it made for you. I'd meant to invite you out to dinner this evening, propose by candlelight, and then hold you in my arms all night. But one look at you in Marc's arms this morning and I——'

'I wasn't in his arms,' she protested, sitting up. 'He guessed something had happened between us while we were away and he was trying to find out the details.'

'Which you refused to tell him,' Reed laughed softly. 'Poor Marc.'

'The man is a menace!'

'True,' Reed nodded. 'But he does care for you in his own way. He told me that if I hurt you again he would break both my legs!'

'He doesn't have the energy!' Darcy derided.

'No,' Reed smiled, his gaze warm on her flushed face. 'I do love you, Darcy,' he told her intensely. 'Being without you the last few days has been like being without a part of myself; the most important part. I need you with me all the time, Darcy.'

She felt the same way, but she frowned her puzzlement. 'How can you say that when you told me I could no longer work for you?'

He gave a rueful grimace. 'Jealousy,' he told her simply.

'Of what? Who?' She gazed up at him dazedly.

'Darcy, you have to realise that until today I had no idea how you felt about me. I was going to propose, but I had no idea if you would accept. Hell, you were dating Marc before we went to Florida,' he scowled. 'I didn't want you anywhere near him.'

'He's just a friend,' she frowned. 'He's always been a friend.'

'He's also a man; a very attractive one, I've been told. Mainly by him!' Reed derided. 'From the first night we met I was attracted to you. God, that isn't completely true; it was so much more than just attraction! For years I had watched my father with my mother, and——'

'I know the way I forget things gets you down,' she put in hastily. 'But I will try——'

'You don't understand, Darcy.' He shook his head. 'For years I watched my father adore my mother *because* of the way she is, not in spite of it. Do you have any idea how difficult it is, in this age of women's liberation, to find a woman you can feel protective towards? It may be old-fashioned, but that's the way I feel about you. The way my father felt about my mother.' A gentle smile curved his lips. 'We all adore my mother, she's the most lovable woman I know. Or, at least, she was. Darcy Faversham soon came first in my heart.'

'You acted as if you couldn't stand the sight of both of us the day your mother arrived in England,' Darcy remembered indignantly. She was willing, if Reed said he did, to accept that he loved her now, but that day Maud arrived he had been rude and insulting to both of them.

'That was because Marc had invited me to the surprise party *he* was giving for your birthday and my mother's arrival had meant my own plans to invite you out alone for a quiet dinner were impossible.' He frowned darkly. 'I was angry at everyone that day. The next day was no better—I imagined you had spent the night with Marc. Knowing how you felt about your own family I knew it wasn't the best time for you to meet mine, but I had to get you away from Marc somehow. But I could see my family overwhelmed you from the start——'

'Not overwhelmed exactly,' she corrected softly. 'Since—after my breakdown I've had difficulty coping with crowds, that's all.'

'And my family is more like a mob!' he derided.

'They're nice people,' she assured him. 'And it isn't families I'm nervous of, Reed, it's just groups of people *per se*. But I'm slowly getting better, coping more. I haven't visited my own parents much the last few months because of— well, because of memories. But I'm slowly learning to deal with them, too.'

'Knowing nothing of what happened at the bank, I assumed when you first came to work for me that your disturbed emotional state was due to a man. Jason.' He sighed. 'I decided to give you the space to get over it——'

'Reed, there's something about Jason I think you should know,' she cut in forcefully.

'The only thing I need to know about him is that he was too stupid to realise what a wonderful woman you are,' he dismissed with a scowl. 'His loss is my gain. But we have to go back a bit in this conversation,' he frowned. 'You really like my family?'

The subject of Jason was far from over, she knew that if she were going to marry Reed. But she was content to settle the other misunderstandings between them before they broached the painful subject of Jason again.

'I like them very much,' she nodded. 'My own parents are good people, too; they're going to love meeting you.' After the years of worrying about her, she knew her parents were going to be ecstatic that she had found happiness at last.

'Marc's right, you know, I am an idiot.' Reed was angry with himself. 'I took your aversion to talking about your home and family to mean you preferred being alone; the fact that for a long time you still didn't date seemed to confirm it. Even when you told me what happened to the woman you worked with at the bank——'

'Jayne,' she put in dully.

'That didn't seem to be a reason to stop visiting your family.' He shook his head. 'So I assumed you just preferred to be on your own. I could accept that until this business with Chris blew up in my face.' He looked grim. 'I'd been hoping that once you got over the man who had hurt you, you would eventually turn to me, but the longer the thing went on in America the more I felt those invisible strings of family commitment

I had been trying to avoid pulling me back there. It came to a point where I knew I couldn't avoid them any longer, and when my mother decided to go on a cruise I realised it was a good time to go and sort the whole sorry mess out. I also wanted to get you away from Marc, if only for a few days. He's an attractive son-of-a——'

'I told you,' she interrupted, 'I like him very much as a friend.'

Reed didn't look mollified. 'He's been walking a dangerously thin line by dating you, and he knew it, too, damn him.'

'He has a very warped sense of humour,' Darcy smiled. 'But no doubt he'll fall in love one day just like the rest of us.'

'I pity the poor woman!'

'I think I rather envy her,' Darcy said slowly.

'Darcy!'

She kissed Reed lightly on the mouth at the sound of his outraged growl. 'I only meant that Marc has a great capacity for loving which he won't allow to go free. I think there's a lot more to him than he allows most of us to see.'

'If there is he's a better actor than I gave him credit for,' Reed derided. 'But enough about him,' he grated jealously.

'You were talking about Florida,' she prompted indulgently.

He nodded ruefully. 'I wanted you to like my family, to get used to them in easy stages——'

'Ease me into them.' She nodded.

'Yes,' he admitted drily. 'Instead of which you

were thrown into the midst of them on our arrival like a tasty morsel to a pack of wolves!'

'That's too extreme, Reed,' she chided softly. 'Besides, maybe it was exactly what I needed to take me completely out of the world I had retreated into——'

'Shock treatment?' Reed derided.

'Rupert told me that if I wanted to get completely better I had to meet life head-on, and I thought that by coming to London to live I had done that. Instead I'd just pushed all the unpleasantness to the back of my mind, made another "safe" world for myself here. I wasn't really living, Reed.'

He looked at her anxiously. 'And you are now?'

She nodded. 'I'm getting there.'

'I thought so today when you stormed into my office and told me exactly what you thought of me,' he said admiringly. 'You were like a lioness fighting for her mate. In the past you've always taken the passive way out, refused to fight even when you knew something was yours—as I am. I could have made love to you right there in my office if we hadn't had such a shocked audience.' He gave a self-derisive smile. 'Roy now thinks I'm the biggest bastard he's ever met!'

'We'll invite him to the wedding.' Darcy snuggled against him.

'You really will marry me?' He looked down at her almost uncertainly.

'I'm a lioness, remember.' She growled low in her throat. 'You're mine now, Reed Hunter. And I'm keeping you.'

'I think the family would lynch me if you didn't marry me,' he admitted ruefully. 'They all think you're wonderful. I have strict instructions not to return without you!'

She sobered. 'How are Chris and Diane?'

He sighed. 'Shaky, but the foundations are still standing. I've loaned Diane the money and she's going to become Chris's partner. They'll make it.'

Darcy felt her heart swell with love for this man at the way he had arranged to help Chris without stripping him of his pride; Diane would make a wonderful business partner for her husband.

'Chris insisted on telling the rest of the family what he had done,' Reed continued abruptly. 'I admire him for that.' His voice was gruff with emotion.

'And the others?' Darcy looked at him anxiously.

'We're a family, Darcy,' he grimaced. 'We squabble among ourselves, but Lord help any danger that threatens any of us.'

'I can't wait to be included in that loving warmth.' She gave him a glowing smile.

'*You* will be my family, Darcy,' he told her intently. 'You will always come first.'

She knew that, was sure of his love when she learnt how patiently he had waited to court her; he wasn't a man known for his restraint. There had been so many misunderstandings. But there was only one left of real importance now. She shied away from it, but knew it had to be faced.

'What is it?' Reed demanded sharply, searching the cloudy unhappiness of her eyes.

'We have to talk about Jason,' she told him regretfully.

Anger flared in his eyes. 'He isn't important, Darcy——'

'Reed, I haven't told you all there is to know about him,' she cut in forcefully, pulling out of his arms to stand up, avoiding his gaze as she thrust her hands into the pockets of her skirt. 'You know that I worked briefly as a family helper.' She could feel Reed's tension now as he sat on the edge of his seat. 'Well it was to a widower and his three children.'

'Jason?'

'Yes.'

'He took advantage of you while you were working in his house——'

'No!' she heatedly denied the harsh accusation. 'I—I wasn't exactly working for him——'

'You were living with him?' Reed frowned darkly.

'Yes,' she confirmed raggedly.

'But you——'

'I was a virgin when you made love to me,' she acknowledged impatiently. 'I told you the reason for that.' She moistened her lips. 'I—The bank kept me on during my breakdown, I was classed as—sick.' The memory was painful to Darcy. 'It was a year before I felt able to walk in the door of the bank again—and I walked out again two minutes later. I couldn't bear to be in there where it happened. I walked and walked after that,

needing to talk to someone but sure everyone was
sick of listening to me——'

'I'm sure that isn't true!'

'Probably not,' she acknowledged huskily. 'But
it didn't help me at the time. Then as I walked
around the lake in the local park I saw Vicky,
Jayne's oldest child.' She swallowed hard. 'She
was only ten at the time, and I didn't think she
should be there on her own. I stopped to talk to
her. Her grandmother had moved in to take care
of them since—the last year, but she had fallen
down and broken her hip, and was in hospital
before going on to convalesce. Their father had to
work to support them all, so Vicky and her
younger sister and brother had become latch-key
children.'

'Then Jason is——'

'Jayne's husband,' she revealed shakily, looking
up at him challengingly, daring him to condemn
her as so many people had when she had moved
into the Summers' home to take care of the three
children and their father.

Reed swallowed convulsively, breathing out
raggedly before striding across the room to pull
her into his arms and cradle her against his chest.
'My darling. My poor, poor darling.' His voice
was pained in her curls.

The tears flowed freely. 'The gossip started
straight away, speculation as to whether or not
we had been having an affair before Jayne died,
things like that,' she told him shakily. 'We
weren't!'

'I know that.'

She could tell that he did, that he had never thought it for a moment. 'We all tried to ignore it, knew it wasn't true. And then—then one night Jason said that as everyone believed it anyway, why didn't we just go ahead and have an affair! He—He's attractive enough, a nice man, I felt an obligation——'

'Oh, Darcy!' Reed's tears mingled with her own as he held her to him fiercely.

'He tried. It—I—He couldn't do it. He cried afterwards, and as I held him I cried, too. It was all such a mess. We couldn't even look at each other after that,' she continued shakily. 'The children were becoming sensitive to the tension between us, and I—I agreed with Jason when he said he thought it best if he got someone else in until his mother returned.'

'And when you saw him again this time?' Reed prompted gruffly.

She smiled through her tears. 'He told me he's met a nice woman, she gets on well with all the children, and they're getting married soon. She isn't Jayne, but he loves her.'

'I'm happy for him,' Reed told her with feeling. 'And for you.'

She gave a choked sob. 'I've been so afraid of telling you about him, frightened you would be disgusted by what I had done.'

He framed her face with gentle hands as he looked deeply into her eyes. 'Nothing you could ever do would disgust me, least of all what you tried to do for Jason. If it's possible, I love you more than I did before.'

'Hold me, Reed,' she pleaded shakily. 'Just hold me!'

'For the rest of our lives,' he promised.

'What are you doing, Reed?' she protested as he put his hands over her eyes.

'Wait and see,' he teased.

After leaving Marc's studio Reed had insisted on taking her back to his apartment. Darcy had teased him about showing her his etchings; with his hands over her eyes as he guided her inside she wasn't so sure that that wasn't what he was doing!

'There,' he said with satisfaction, removing his hands.

It took her a few seconds to adjust her eyesight to the dimly lit room, the glow from the cabinet on the far wall seeming to be the only illumination. Darcy was drawn to it like a magnet.

Unicorns, hundreds of them, made from glass, wood, plaster, each design different from the last, filled the entire cabinet.

Reed's arms came around her waist from behind as he bent to lay his cheek beside hers. 'Unicorns have always been very special to me. Beautiful, unique, magical, like the woman I love,' he murmured throatily. 'I could only share the gift of one with someone like her.'

'Everyone else knew that,' she realised breathlessly, fascinated by the creature bathed in such mystical beauty.

'You remind me of the unicorn.' He kissed the creamy length of her throat. 'But you're real for me, so very real. May I?' He slipped the necklace around her throat that she had flung down in front of him earlier.

'Please,' she said with feeling, understanding at last.

He turned her in his arms. 'Do you still distrust my gift to you?'

He was giving her so much more than the unicorn, she knew that now, knew he was giving her the dreams and love that went with it. She reached up to gently caress his mouth with hers. 'I love you, Reed.' She looked at him with tear-filled eyes.

'It's all I've ever wanted,' he told her shakily.

They gazed into each others' eyes, words no longer necessary as they made their vows for a lifetime.

'I have another gift for you.' Reed dragged himself back from the magical depths of her eyes with effort.

'I only need you, Reed,' she assured him throatily.

Amusement lightened his expression. 'You might need this on occasion!'

Her eyes narrowed at his teasing. 'What is it?'

He moved to switch on the main light in the room, picking up a parcel from the coffee table to hold it out to her. 'Open it,' he invited softly.

She looked at him suspiciously for several minutes but could read nothing from his expression. But he was enjoying himself at her expense, she knew that. And after the tension of the day a little levity would be welcome, although she didn't reveal that as she warily unwrapped the oblong parcel.

'Oh, Reed!' She choked back her laughter as she looked inside the box.

'Do you like it?'

'I love it!' Her laughter couldn't be contained as she stared down at the beautifully made glass slipper.

His arms moved about her waist. 'I intend to take it along whenever we go out to dinner!' he teased her.

'My Prince Charming!' Her hands linked at the back of his head as she moulded her body to his, completely sure of his love with this last romantic gesture towards her forgetfulness.

'I don't think what I'm feeling right now could ever be included in a fairy tale!'

She could feel his arousal against her. 'Let's go to bed,' she invited.

'You see,' he grinned, 'I knew you were made for me!'

CHAPTER ELEVEN

'Darcy?'

'Mmm?'

'How much do you love me?'

'I moved to America with you, didn't I?'

'And became aunty to Linda and Wade's twins, Mike and Marie's two, and Chris and Diane's one point five, I know. But tell me how much you love me, Darcy.'

'Why?'

'Just answer the question!'

'It depends.'

'On what?'

'On whether you're after something or you're leading up to an invitation to go home to bed.'

'Both.'

'Ah. In that case, I love you very much.'

'Good.'

'Reed?'

'Hmm?'

'It's five minutes since you asked; I'm waiting for the invitation.'

'We can leave as soon as you've paid the bill for dinner.'

'As soon as *I* have? But—Reed, do you suppose it's catching?'

'I hope not, I don't think I'd look quite as beautiful as you do carrying around that lump.'

'That "lump" happens to be our son or daughter!'

'I know. And I love it already. I'm glad you forgot to take your pills——'

'*I* didn't forget anything, you were in charge at the time. And don't think this diversion is going to make me overlook the fact that you've forgotten your wallet, because it isn't!'

'If you hadn't been doing shameless things to my body just before we left home I wouldn't have forgotten it!'

'Are you complaining?'

'Hell, no! God, Darcy, no one can say you don't fight for what you want now!'

'Only for the man who believes in unicorns and glass slippers and made me believe in them, too.'

'You say the damnedest things! Let's get out of here.'

'Yes, Reed.'

'I want you to say it just like that when we get home.'

'Yes, Reed.'

'*Just* like that, Darcy!'

'As soon as I've settled the bill . . .'

'Darcy?'

'Mmm?'

'Do you have both shoes on?'

'If I don't I'm sure you'll deal with it.'

'Your wish is my command.'

'Really?'
'Darcy!'
'Yes, Reed.'

Harlequin Presents

Coming Next Month

Available in January wherever paperback books are sold, or through Harlequin Reader Service:

In the U.S.
P.O. Box 1397
Buffalo, N.Y.
14240-1397

In Canada
P.O. Box 603
Fort Erie, Ontario
L2A 9Z9

Now Available!
Buy all three books in
MAURA SEGER'S fabulous trilogy!

EYE OF THE STORM

ECHO OF THUNDER

EDGE OF DAWN

Be a part of the Callahan and Gargano families as they live and love through the most turbulent decades in history!

"...should be required reading for every American."

Romantic Times

To order all three books please send your name, address and zip or postal code along with a check or money order for $12.15 (includes 75¢ for postage and handling) made payable to Worldwide Library Reader Service to:

WORLDWIDE LIBRARY READER SERVICE

In the U.S.:	In Canada:
P.O. Box 1397	5770 Yonge St., P.O. Box 2800
Buffalo, N.Y.	Postal Station A
14240-1397	Willowdale, Ontario M2N 6J3

PLEASE SPECIFY BOOK TITLES WITH YOUR ORDER.

TRL-H-1

Here's how to get this special offer from Harlequin!

December
BETTY NEELS TREASURY EDITION COUPON

As simple as 1...2...3!

1. **Each month, save one Treasury Edition coupon from your favorite Romance or Presents novel.**
2. **In four months you'll have saved four Treasury Edition coupons (only one coupon per month allowed).**
3. **Then all you have to do is fill out and return the order form provided, along with the four Treasury Edition coupons required and $2.95 for postage and handling.**

Mail to: **Harlequin Reader Service**

In the U.S.A.	In Canada
901 Fuhrmann Blvd.	P.O. Box 609
P.O. Box 1397	Fort Erie, Ontario
Buffalo, NY 14240	L2A 9Z9

BN-Dec-2

Please send me my Special copy of the Betty Neels Treasury Edition. I have enclosed the four Treasury Edition coupons required and $2.95 for postage and handling along with this order form. (Please Print)

NAME_____

ADDRESS_____

CITY_____

STATE/PROV._____ ZIP/POSTAL CODE_____

SIGNATURE_____

This offer is limited to one order per household.

SUPPLIES LIMITED

This special Betty Neels offer expires February 28, 1987.

Janet Dailey
Americana

Don't miss a single title from this great collection. The first eight titles have already been published. Complete and mail this coupon today to order books you may have missed.

Harlequin Reader Service

In U.S.A.
901 Fuhrmann Blvd.
P.O. Box 1397
Buffalo, N.Y. 14140

In Canada
P.O. Box 2800
Postal Station A
5170 Yonge Street
Willowdale, Ont. M2N 6J3

Please send me the following titles from the Janet Dailey Americana Collection. I am enclosing a check or money order for $2.75 for each book ordered, plus 75¢ for postage and handling.

_____	ALABAMA	Dangerous Masquerade
_____	ALASKA	Northern Magic
_____	ARIZONA	Sonora Sundown
_____	ARKANSAS	Valley of the Vapours
_____	CALIFORNIA	Fire and Ice
_____	COLORADO	After the Storm
_____	CONNECTICUT	Difficult Decision
_____	DELAWARE	The Matchmakers

Number of titles checked @ $2.75 each = $_____

N.Y. RESIDENTS ADD
   APPROPRIATE SALES TAX $_____

Postage and Handling $___.75___

                    TOTAL $_____

I enclose _____

(Please send check or money order. We cannot be responsible for cash sent through the mail.)

PLEASE PRINT

NAME _____

ADDRESS _____

CITY _____

STATE/PROV. _____

BLJD-A-1